SWEET SURRENDER

JILL SANDERS

GRAYTON

This is a work of fiction. Names, characters, places, and incidents either are the product of the author's imagination or are used fictitiously, and any resemblance to actual persons, living or dead, business establishments, events, or locales is entirely coincidental.

SWEET SURRENDER

DIGITAL ISBN: 978-1-945100-16-1

PRINT ISBN: 979-8-647120-17-5

SUMMARY

Bella Rothschild has finally done it. She's hit the big time. Being a music star was all she'd ever wanted, but with her new fame and the release of her second album comes a lack of privacy. After a few credible and scary threats, she decides to hide away in the small town of Silver Cove until things blow over. The last thing she expects is to fall for the hired help.

Calvin has worked hard his entire life to get where he is. As the new manager of the Haven Resorts, he's built up his reputation as a man of his word. So, when he promises the sexy starlet the privacy and protection of the resort, he'll make sure she gets it. Even if it means guarding the pretty brunette himself.

*B*ella opened the email once more and read it again slowly as the plane took off. She felt a shiver run down her spine when she got to the part about signing the contract with Sunflower Records. She was officially going to be an artist.

Here she was, her eighteenth birthday only three weeks behind her, and she had made it. Or was about to, at least.

Her brother Ben had had a hand in making this happen, but for the most part, it was her hard work and talent that had gotten her this far.

Now, she just needed to rely on that talent to carry her through her first record deal.

Maggie, her agent, was going to be meeting her at the airport in Atlanta where they would travel to LA together. She'd signed on with Maggie Harris, one of the top vocal agents, shortly after her brother had introduced them when the woman had been staying at her sisters-in-law's elite resort, East Haven.

Bella had moved out of her parents' home shortly after her sixteenth birthday and moved in with her brother and his new wife, Sarah, in their brand-new home. And she'd never been happier.

As her brother knew firsthand, their parents could be a little—okay, a lot—to handle.

They had actually wanted to ship her off to Europe somewhere for school. Back then, she'd been sure it was because they hated her. But now she understood it was because she had been more than they had wanted to handle at the time.

Her father's career and her mother's social life had been their priority, not raising their "oops" child.

She'd been even more hardheaded as a child than her brother had been and had been determined to have things her way. So, naturally, when she'd found out that they were about to ship her away, she'd run away. Straight into the arms of her brother. Thankfully, he'd taken her in and fought for her.

Spending two years with Ben and Sarah had been wonderful. She'd gone to school at Brighton, a private school. Ben and Sarah ran Elite Resorts International and East Haven, an exclusive resort on a private island off the coast of Maine. Elite Resorts was a business their father had desperately wanted to sink his teeth into all his life.

Since Sarah had inherited the lucrative business from her late grandfather, Bella's parents had focused all their attention on their only son and their new daughter-in-law, instead of their only daughter.

She'd talked to them only a handful of times since moving out and had only seen them twice, during holidays. Ben and Sarah played nice to them but kept them at arm's length. They were wise to their tactics.

Bella smiled down at the email once more. She figured that the path laid out in front of her would dim the hurt and pain of being shunned by her folks.

She didn't need them. The only family she needed she

had, and they supported her one hundred percent. After all, Sarah and Ben had bought her the plane tickets and had helped her arrange for the apartment in LA. In the two years that she'd lived with them, they had given her far more personally and emotionally than her parents had in the sixteen years she'd lived under their roof.

Now, because of her brother and Sarah, she knew she could handle being on her own in California, starting her career as a singer and becoming a star. She told herself that once she stepped foot in LA, she would never think about her parents again.

Four years later...

Bella stepped off the boat and took a deep breath. How had she forgotten how fresh salt air smelled? Closing her eyes for a moment, she enjoyed the sounds of the seagulls floating overhead and the water lapping at the rocks under the dock. More importantly, no vehicles were blasting their horns.

"Are you okay?" JT Thomas asked her. She'd known the man since first coming to Silver Cove. She'd been shocked to find out that he was one of her favorite authors, the infamous JT Whistler. Some of his horror stories had kept her up at night before she'd met him and now one of his latest books was tucked in her suitcase. She'd almost finished it on her flight and had every intention of finishing it later that night. Even if it meant staying up late.

"Yes." She smiled up at him. "I heard you're a father now." She picked up her small backpack, leaving the larger bags for the crew at Holley Hall to take up to the main lodge in their carts.

JT's smile tripled, if there was such a thing. "Yes." His

chest puffed out slightly. "Twins. They just had their first birthday last month." He laughed. "Who would have thought…" He whipped out his phone and showed her a picture of two sleeping babies.

"A boy and girl." She took his phone and looked at the kids closer. "She looks like you."

"Sophia and Liam," he added with a smile.

"Sophia looks like you, Liam takes after Emma. How is she doing by the way?" Bella asked.

"Great," he answered when she handed him back his phone. "Enjoying having me working the ferry again and out of the house two days a week." He chuckled.

"Getting underfoot?" she asked.

"No. Apparently, I keep waking the kids up. Checking on them too much." He shrugged.

"Well, I for one am glad you were here to greet me and take me to the island." She touched his arm.

"Had enough of your brother and sister-in-law?" he asked.

"No, I'm planning on telling them I'm in town later tonight," she admitted.

That stopped him. "They don't know yet?" JT's tone turned worried and he glanced around.

"What?" she asked.

"It's just… last time I knew something before Sarah…" Bella remembered that JT had known Sarah his entire life. "She about skinned me." He wiped the sweat from the back of his neck. Since Bella had known him, JT had kept his blond hair long, but now it was cut shorter, and she wondered if it was because of the kids or the summer heat.

"Then don't tell her you know," she joked as she touched his arm. She walked off the dock just as a golf cart came rolling up to the end of the dock.

She squinted behind her sunglasses and shielded her face

from the sun with her free hand to get a better look at who was driving. Then she stopped.

"What's he doing here?" she asked quietly. JT shifted her bags under his arms and glanced up. She hadn't let him take her guitar case from her, since his hands had been full with her other luggage.

"Oh, that's Calvin. He runs the place now." JT continued down the dock.

She'd known Calvin Winters for what seemed like her entire life. The man was her brother's best friend. She'd only met him personally a handful of times back in her preteen years, when Ben and he had been going to the same boarding school. Back when she'd been an awkward teen with pimples, uncontrollable hair, and skinny legs that were too long for her body.

She'd had a crush on him from the moment she'd laid eyes on the picture Ben had sent of the pair of them at school.

The first time she'd met him was the year he'd tagged along with Ben on their summer vacation, when his parents had had something to deal with and hadn't wanted their son around. Calvin had gone along with their family to Cancun for two weeks. He'd been a broody thirteen-year-old and Bella's nine-year-old heart had been lost instantly. The entire trip, he'd barely said two words to her, but she'd lost her heart all the same.

She watched now as Calvin easily helped JT load her luggage into the back of the golf cart. The two men chatted casually as they went along.

She had felt the pull of sexual desire from plenty of men over the years, but none like what she'd experienced for Calvin.

Squaring her shoulders, she made her way slowly to the foot of the dock. She tried to focus on the dragonflies buzzing the water near the shoreline instead of the man watching her as if she were walking down a catwalk instead of the old dock.

"Hi." She stopped and removed her glasses as he took her smaller bag from her hands.

"Miss Rothschild." He nodded. "When I noticed your name on the registration, I thought it best to greet you myself." He glanced back at the boat. "Your brother didn't come with you?" He was treating her as if he'd never met her before. Did he even remember her? Maybe he didn't? After all, it had been over six years since she'd last seen him.

He hadn't changed much except for the slight dusting of dark hair over his chin and those new muscles she could see through his dress shirt. And he looked taller than he had before.

"No." She frowned. "Why would he?"

He shook his head quickly. "No reason." He reached for her guitar case, but she shook her head.

"I've got this." She moved over to set it down on the seat in the golf cart.

His dark eyebrows rose slightly, but then he nodded and watched her. When she turned back to him, he shifted his gaze as the sound of a boat motor sounded in the distance.

"Shit." JT groaned and tried to shrink behind Bella.

She glanced over, and her shoulders sagged slightly when she noticed Ben, Sarah, and Aurora standing at the helm of the boat as it docked next to the ferry. Her sister-in-law was holding Luna in her arms. Bella had last seen the two-year-old on her first birthday. The mass of fluffy blonde hair the girl had was now in short little braids.

Aurora, her oldest niece, was a few months shy of her fifth birthday. Both of Bella's nieces were dressed in blue-flowered jumpers and white sandals and had white ribbons in their braided hair.

"You have to stick up for me," JT said behind her back. "Tell them I had nothing to do with…" He stopped talking when Sarah rushed over and grabbed her in a big hug as she shifted Luna in her arms slightly so she didn't smoosh the little girl between them.

"You're here," her sister-in-law said, holding onto her while Ben helped Aurora out of the boat. The four-year-old was very independent and trying to push her father's helping hands away.

"I am." She smiled. "I was going to call…" she started, but Sarah waved her off after she released her.

"We're surprised, not upset that you didn't call us." Sarah ran her eyes over Bella. "I can see the fear in your eyes." Sarah chuckled. "Really, I'm not mad at you." Her eyes moved to JT and Calvin quickly, and Bella noticed both men shrink slightly.

It had only been a year since her brother and his family had visited her in LA, but still, Bella could see the slight changes in her sister-in-law and her brother.

Sarah set Luna down, and Bella was surprised to see the girl run up and down the dock on her own now.

She was pretty steady for a two-year-old, but Ben was still less than a foot away from both his daughters, hands at the ready in case either of them ventured too close to the edge.

"Hey." Ben finally made it to her side. Aurora tucked herself behind her father's leg as she looked up at her while Luna continued to jabber and play with a stuffed dog she had been holding onto as she plopped down at her father's feet.

"Hi," Bella said to her brother. She bent down to get on her niece's level. "Hi, Aurora, do you remember me?" Before she could finish speaking, the little girl was shaking her head from side to side. Then her big blue eyes moved beyond Bella and grew larger.

"Cal!" the little girl cried out and released her death hold on her father's leg. She rushed past Bella to jump into the man's waiting arms.

Instantly, Luna glanced up and giggled. "Cal!" she mimicked her older sister and tried to get to her feet. Ben helped her, but instead of letting her rush to the man, he picked her up and held onto her himself.

"There she is." Calvin chuckled and spun Aurora around in circles. "My favorite lady."

"More," Aurora giggled.

"This is why I don't bring them here often. I think they have both fallen in love. Especially, Aurora." Ben sighed and reached over to wrap his free arm around Bella. "Hey," he said again, "how long are you here for?"

She closed her eyes and held onto her brother. Not wanting to tell him that she didn't know herself, she threw out a number.

"Two weeks." She placed a careful smile on her face before pulling away. "I thought it would be easier to stay…"

"Of course." Ben squeezed her shoulder. "You don't have to stay at our place. You're welcome anywhere." Her brother's eyes moved up to where Calvin was still swinging Aurora in circles. "I take it you have my little sister all set up?"

Calvin instantly stopped moving, keeping the giggling Aurora hanging upside down in his arms so that he could talk freely. "Yes, she's all set up in the Summer Suite."

Bella noticed how much more relaxed the man was now that Ben was there.

"I don't need…" She started to argue about being given the largest room in the entire resort, but Sarah stepped forward and nudged her to start walking beside her on the pathway.

"The men will take your things and the girls inside." She

motioned to the huge white building that loomed in the distance.

Bella fell into step with Sarah easily. She'd liked her from the moment she'd met her a few years back. Who wouldn't? Sarah was so down to earth and friendly.

But where Sarah shined, her mother Crystal exploded. When she'd met Crystal Holley for the first time, she'd been welcomed into a new world. Both Sarah and her mother had this way about them that put everyone around them at ease.

Bella had been going through some really tough times when she'd first escaped to Silver Cove. She hadn't known how to act around either of the women, having never really experienced a mother figure. It wasn't as if her mother, Juliette, had filled that role at any point in Bella's young life.

"So," Sarah broke into her thoughts, "tell me what's going on."

"What makes you think…" Sarah tugged her to a stop by pulling lightly on her elbow. The look she gave Bella had her sighing. She should have known better. There was no way she could keep her voice or her eyes from giving her troubles away. It was the main reason she'd wanted to avoid seeing them until later. She'd hoped to have a few days to recover from the scare before seeing her family.

"Something's up." Sarah nudged her aside on the walking path until they sat on a stone bench under a large apple tree. "I know that your brother may be blind when it comes to you being unhappy, but I have eyes." She smiled over at her. "You can tell me."

"I know." Bella closed her eyes and took a few deep breaths. "I was hoping for a few days to collect my thoughts—"

"Does it have something to do with Shane?" Sarah asked.

"Who?" Bella's eyes narrowed as she frowned. Then she

remembered the man she'd been dating last year and shook her head and chuckled. "That lasted a hot minute."

"Oh, good." Sarah sighed. "I didn't like the guy."

"You and Ben never like anyone…" She stopped herself. "Never mind."

"None of them were ever good enough for you." Sarah picked up her hand and turned it over. "It's written right here." She ran a fingertip up a line on her palm.

Bella laughed. "You never believed in all the mumbo jumbo your mother believes in. Why start?"

"Palm reading is mumbo jumbo, except when it comes to love." She glanced up at her, then added in a thick gypsy accent, "I see a kind man in your future…"

"Just what I want," Bella added sarcastically.

"Shush." Sarah waved the comment away and continued. "A man you did not expect will come into your life and…" Sarah's eyes narrowed as she bent over her palm. "Shield you from… the darkness that is looming over you."

Bella felt a shiver race down her spine.

"You can read all that in my hand?" she asked, a little scared at the tone Sarah had taken when she mentioned the darkness.

"That"—Sarah fell back into her own voice—"and in your eyes." She smiled. "So, if it's not a man, then what has that lost look in your eyes? I know that the new record deal is going well, because I read all the gossip magazines." She chuckled at the face Bella gave her. "I know, don't believe everything you see in those, but still…"

"Yes, the second record deal is going great. I actually just wrapped up recording and have a few weeks off before they want me to start touring again."

"Great, so…" Sarah waited. "What has you so down?"

"I guess I'm just tired." Bella glanced away and took in all the flowers that surrounded them. The gardens at East

Haven Resort were almost legendary. Even after Rodney, the old groundskeeper, passed away, they continued to bloom and grow under the new groundskeeper, Kevin.

She could hear guests of the resort enjoying themselves out near the pool and relaxed.

Sarah was silent for a while. "I'm here, you know, if you decide you want to talk."

"Thanks." She turned and pasted another smile on her face. "But what I want more than anything is some peace and quiet away from the demands of being a star."

"You're a star." Sarah smiled. "It amazes us every day how far you've come. You knew what you wanted and went after it."

"Kind of like you and Ben," Bella said. "You two are great together."

Her sister-in-law's smile slipped.

"We had a big fight this morning." Sarah leaned back on the bench. "It's my fault."

"What happened?" Bella instantly worried.

"I couldn't find Luna's blanket. The one you gave her. It's her favorite, and she never goes anywhere without it. She was screaming and..." She closed her eyes. "I cussed." Her eyes flew open. "In front of her."

Bella couldn't help it, she laughed. "Well, damn."

Sarah's eyes narrowed. "We are trying not to say those words in front of her."

Bella tilted her head. "Did your mother cuss in front of you when you were a child?"

Sarah rolled her eyes. "So many people cussed in front of me. Along with doing a bunch of other things."

"Okay," she said slowly. "You turned out okay, right?"

"I'd like to think so."

"Then I don't think words, bad or good, are going to turn your daughters into serial killers or drug dealers."

Sarah was silent for a while. "I know you're right." She rested her head back and looked up through the leaves of the apple tree. "Still, I had hoped to give my kids much better childhoods than I had."

Bella took her sister-in-law's hands in hers. "Then simply love them. Trust me, it's the most important thing in the world."

Sarah smiled. "I'm sorry. Here I was trying to unburden you from your problems but instead I loaded you down with my own."

Bella laughed. "No, hearing them actually made me feel much better. Life goes on." She stood up and stretched. "Now, I think I want to unpack and take a dip in the pool. Then I'm going to gorge myself on Adam's dinner and desserts before I crawl into bed and sleep for two days straight."

"Don't forget the drinks." Sarah laughed as she took her arm. "We have a new bartender." Her voice changed, and she gained another fake accent. "He's from Russia and has this sexy accent." Sarah giggled.

They talked about food and drinks as they made their way up to the resort. When they stepped inside, Ben, Aurora, Luna, and Calvin were all waiting for them just inside the front doors.

Calvin had switched to giving Luna his attention, and the little girl was eating it up.

"Your luggage has been taken up to your rooms. Would you care for anything to eat or drink?" Calvin asked and, for a moment, she got lost in his sexy voice. He didn't need an accent to make her practically drool over him. He handed her a key and waited for her answer.

"No, thank you." She had expected him to leave, but he continued to stand there, holding Luna against his chest with Aurora attached to his leg as if they both belonged there.

Trying to ignore the hunk, and all the old feelings that were flooding her mind, she turned to her brother. "I was going to hit the pool before dinner," she said easily. "Care to join in the fun?"

"We had promised the girls a dip and brought our swimsuits along." He nodded to a backpack he'd thrown over his shoulder.

"Great." She smiled and glanced towards the stairs. "I'll go change and meet you at the pool." She made her way up the wide staircase while avoiding Calvin's gaze.

Stepping into the Summer Suite, she leaned against the door and took a couple of deep breaths. She hadn't thought it would be this hard keeping a secret from her family.

Her bags sat just inside the doorway. Picking up the smallest one, which held her swimsuit, she made her way across the sitting room and into the bedroom. She'd only been in this room once before, when she'd visited Sarah and Ben during one of their weekends stays when she'd lived with them.

The Summer Suite had two full-sized bedrooms and bathrooms with a large sitting room between them. It was way too big for just her, but she wasn't going to complain. She technically didn't know how long she was going to be staying there or if her agent, Maggie, would be visiting during her stay.

Tossing the bag on the king-sized bed, she pulled out her swimsuit and changed quickly. Being at East Haven Resort was one of her fondest memories growing up, even though the first time she'd visited the place had been a few weeks after her sixteenth birthday.

She pulled a light cover-up on over her swimsuit and decided to braid her hair. When she stepped into the massive bathroom, she gasped at the beauty.

The last time she'd been in the rooms, she hadn't seen the

bathroom. She had never seen anything so wonderful before. The bathtub was as big as a hot tub with a huge glass shower on one end and a gas fireplace with a flat screen television above it along the other end.

A long shallow trough-like sink with two faucets filled the opposite wall. A huge lighted mirror hung over it all.

There was a small wood door and, when she peeked her head in, she realized it was a sauna. Shutting the door, she thought about enjoying that later that evening.

"I could get used to this." She smiled as she stepped into the massive closet. "If only I'd brought more clothes," she joked to herself, remembering the six pieces of luggage sitting in the other room that she'd carted through the airport herself.

Pulling on her sandals again, she picked up her discarded clothes and walked back to the closet to hang them up. The lone shirt and slacks looked so lonely in the massive space. "I'll bring your friends in later," she promised them.

She grabbed her cell phone and made her way downstairs and outside to the larger of the three swimming pools. She wanted to enjoy time with her family, but she knew that the fear and the secrets she was keeping from them would prevent her from relaxing completely.

CHAPTER TWO

Calvin was seriously wondering how far his patience could stretch. First thing that morning, he had found out from Heather, who had heard it from Stacey, that Bella Rothschild had booked a room for the next few weeks.

Of course, he remembered Ben's little sister. How could he forget the summer he'd spent with Ben and his family in Mexico? It had been obvious the girl had a huge crush on him all summer long. He'd done everything to discourage her. After all, it was his best friend's little sister.

He'd known Ben Rothschild, Bella's older brother, since middle school. They had met at the private school in the Alps they had both been shipped off to so that their parents wouldn't have to deal with them.

Both Ben and he had been forgotten children whose parents had spent thousands of dollars for someone else to deal with them. Of course, the similarity of their stories ended there.

Ben had been sent there because his parents were selfish and busy living their lives the way they wanted, and a teenage boy didn't fit into their plans. Calvin had been sent there because of all the trouble he'd caused his family.

Ben had been the only reason he'd been able to claw his way out of the darkness that had consumed him back then.

After graduation, Ben had been lucky enough to get a job at Elite Resorts, thanks to family connections. A few years later, he'd married the granddaughter of Carl Harrison, the owner of the multi-million-dollar business. Then, when the older man had died, Ben's new wife, Sarah had inherited everything from her grandfather. Including East Haven resorts.

The moment Calvin had met Sarah at their wedding a few years back, he'd liked her. She was more down to earth than anyone he would have expected Ben to fall for. Ben had always feared that his parents would arrange his entire life, including who he married.

Two years after Ben and Sarah had married, Calvin had received a phone call from his friend. He'd been happily surprised when he'd been offered a temporary manager job at East Haven. The last manager, Lilith Carriveau, had just given birth to her son, Alex. That was three years ago. Shortly before Sarah's best friend was set to return to the job full time, she'd gotten pregnant again and had her daughter, Brooke.

With the two little ones at home, Sarah had given her a different job so she could stay at home with the children. Which had left the management position open for him.

He'd jumped at the chance to continue working for his friends. After that first year, he had realized that he'd never had a place where he felt like he fit in so well. Even in his own childhood home, he had always felt like a stranger.

Was it one of the reasons he had acted out so badly as a teen? Either way, he knew that if it hadn't been for Ben Roth-schild, he probably wouldn't be alive.

He'd been watching out for the ferry so he could be the one to greet Bella Rothschild himself. He knew Ben and Sarah and their two little girls, Aurora and Luna, wouldn't be far behind.

What he hadn't expected was the fist-to-the-gut attraction he'd felt upon seeing the pretty brunette slowly stroll down the dock towards him. Had she always been this gorgeous? The sunlight hitting her had red hints almost glowing in her hair.

She had been wearing a dark silver tank top with flowing white cotton pants and silver sandals and had walked towards him like she was on a catwalk instead of the old dock. His heart had jumped in his chest when she'd slowly flipped her hair and lowered the sunglasses from her eyes as she smiled at him.

Then, it was as if the entire world stopped. The sadness he'd seen in her dark eyes had made him frown slightly as she talked with JT.

Then Ben and Sarah had arrived, and his attention had been pulled to entertaining their daughters. He loved the little girls and always enjoyed playing with Aurora. Little Luna was just starting to come out of her shell around him. He figured that she was following her big sister, who always hung on him and wanted him to spin her around like an airplane.

After making sure Bella's luggage was delivered up to her room, he stood around the lobby with Ben while Sarah and Bella talked outside.

Ben sighed. "She looks unhappy." He nodded towards the doors while Calvin kept hold of the two little girls.

"Yeah. Any idea why?"

Ben shook his head. "There are rumors about a breakup, but something tells me it's not that."

Calvin shifted Luna in his arms as Aurora weaved

between his legs. "Whatever it is, this is the best place to recover."

"Yeah," Ben agreed as the women stepped inside.

When they all agreed to head to the pool, Calvin figured the least he could do was to ensure them a spot at the larger pool. After everyone went to change into their swimsuits, he rushed to the pool area and asked Ken, the staff member working the area, to set aside a few chairs for the family.

Walking over to the bar, he asked Stacy to make sure the family had whatever drinks they wanted. It helped to give the staff a heads-up that the bosses were present. Even though Sarah and Ben were really relaxed, Calvin prided himself on making sure everything was perfect, as he did for all of the guests.

Then he headed down to the kitchen to see about getting some of the little cheese crackers he knew Aurora liked, along with a fruit and a cheese platter for the adults.

Stepping into the kitchen, he made a point not to get in the way of Adam or any of his staff. He knew the man was very particular with his job and, since the guy made some of the best food in Maine, he tended to stay out of his way.

"Hey, Adam." Calvin got the man's attention. "Just a heads-up, Ben and Sarah are on the grounds. They're heading to the pool with Bella and the girls."

"Bella's here?" The Frenchman's outer shell cracked slightly, and he smiled. Calvin knew the man normally only did that when he was talking about his wife and kids.

"She just arrived. We'll host her for the next two weeks or so. She's in the Summer Suite."

"Bien." Adam set down the pan with a chunk of salmon he'd been preparing. "I'll see to putting something together for them for a snack." He smiled. "I know Aurora likes those cheese crackers."

Calvin chuckled. "I'll deliver those myself." He made his way towards the large pantry.

"You've already won her heart," Adam joked.

Calvin laughed. "It's nice being loved unconditionally." He pulled out the box of crackers and poured a handful into a bowl. "I bet you love it."

Adam chuckled. "Alex was angry with me this morning because I had to go to work." Adam's oldest boy had just turned three a few months back. "They'll be stopping by for lunch." His smile grew. "We just found out number three is on the way."

"What?" Calvin almost dropped the bowl of crackers. "Congratulations." His smile grew as he walked over and shook the man's hand.

"Merci." Adam laughed and shook his hand. "I'll let Lilly know that the family is here. She may bring the kids early so they can play with their cousins."

Calvin had learned early on that even though Lilith and Sarah weren't really related, the two best friends had thought of each other as sisters since Lilith had escaped to Silver Cove from hurricane Katrina when she was a young teenager. She'd lived with Sarah and her mother Crystal Holley before moving onto the island and working at the resort with Sarah.

"I'll take this up. You can send the platter up when it's ready." He nodded to the man as he headed back outside.

When he stepped out into the pool area this time, the family was already there, enjoying the water. It appeared that Bella had arrived just before he had, since she was still covered in a long flowing top and was just setting a bag down next to Sarah's things.

They hadn't seen him yet, and his steps faltered when Bella pulled off the cover-up and rushed to the side of the pool. He smiled when she executed one of the best cannonballs he'd ever witnessed.

He'd had a moment to enjoy the sexy tanned skin wrapped in a silver bikini before she hit the water with a massive splash. Aurora and Luna laughed. He couldn't help but think how much she'd changed since the last time he'd seen her.

"Do it again!" Aurora yelled out.

Bella chuckled. "I'm afraid one is all I have in me." She swam towards the family at the shallow end of the pool.

Then Aurora spotted him. "Calvin, jump in," she called towards him.

"Sorry, princess, I can't right now. But I brought you some of your favorite crackers." He held up the bowl, then set it on the small table next to their chairs.

His eyes kept skirting towards Bella, who was frowning at him and trying to avoid eye contact.

He moved over to the side of the pool as Aurora swam expertly towards him.

"Please?" she asked with a slight frown.

"I'm working. But next time you come to visit I'll show you how to do a proper cannonball," he said with a wink.

"That was a proper one." Bella moved closer to him.

"Oh?" He chuckled and glanced over to Ben. "Your sister hasn't seen either of our cannonballs, has she?"

Ben laughed. "Who do you think taught her?" He nodded to his sister, then shook his head. "But you can't teach perfection." Ben laughed. "Calvin has one of the best cannonballs I've ever witnessed."

"That sounds like a challenge." Bella smirked.

"Consider it one." Calvin stood up and dusted off his slacks. "Adam is sending up a snack platter for you. Lilith and the kids should be along soon." He motioned to the chairs.

"I'll make sure there is plenty of saved space for everyone. We're pretty booked at the moment."

"Thanks," Ben said, shifting Luna in his arms. The kid was holding onto her father tightly. She had yet to learn how to maneuver in the water like her older sister but wasn't afraid of it as she had been last year.

"She's getting better." He motioned to Luna. "I'll wager by the end of the summer she'll be another tadpole like her big sister."

Ben laughed. "We're working on it."

"Thank you, Calvin." Sarah smiled up at him.

"If you need anything…" He nodded to the family and made his way back inside.

For the remainder of the day, he couldn't get his mind off the image of Bella tucking her legs to her chest and jumping into the water with a huge smile on her face. He'd never seen anything sexier in his entire life.

CHAPTER THREE

*S*pending time with her family improved Bella's mood considerably, and she was sure this was the best decision she'd made in a long time.

Just spending an hour in the water with her nieces had lifted the heavy burden from her shoulders. Playing with Aurora and teaching Luna how to swim had worn her out.

Just before lunchtime rolled around, Lilly and her two kids, Alex, who was three, and Brooke, who was the same age as Luna, arrived.

They all sat around the pool area enjoying the lunch that Adam brought up from the kitchen himself. The kids hit the pool again shortly after until it was determined to be their nap time.

After everyone left, she decided to stick it out at the pool and rested back to enjoy the sun and some quiet. She hadn't planned on falling asleep, but sometime later, a shadow fell over her, causing her to jerk awake.

"Sorry." Calvin smiled down at her. "I just came to check up on you." He motioned to the seat next to her and she nodded. "You might want to put some sunblock on soon." He motioned towards her.

She glanced down, but since her eyes had yet to adjust to the light, she shrugged. "I was about to head in," she lied, thankful she had on a pair of dark sunglasses so he couldn't tell that she wasn't fully awake yet or that she'd been asleep in the first place.

"Did you enjoy your visit with your family?" he asked.

"I did." She smiled. "My nieces seem to like you a lot." She shifted to sit up a little.

Hearing Calvin's chuckle had her insides doing little funny flips. God, he'd grown even more sexy over the years. His smile melted her knees and insides.

"I know the way to a woman's heart." He leaned forward. "Cheese crackers." His smile doubled.

She felt her entire body ignite. "They were pretty good," she admitted.

"Adam orders them direct from France." He shrugged and waved to a few guests as they passed by. "I hope everything was to your liking." Her eyebrows shot up in question. "Lunch, that is. Do you need another drink?" He glanced over to her tea, which she'd forgotten about.

"No, thank you. Everything has been wonderful." She glanced out over the pool to the waters of the bay beyond the green grassy yard. "Then again"—she turned her eyes back towards him— "I don't think I've ever been here when things weren't perfect."

He nodded. "If you need anything during your stay…" He started to get up, but she held up her hand to stop him.

"While I'm here…" She swallowed. She needed to talk to him but had wanted to wait until her brother and Sarah weren't around. "I would appreciate the inn's discretion. I'm here to escape and don't want the news to get out that I'm on the island."

He was silent as if thinking about something, but then he nodded in agreement. "You have my word. No one will bother you while you're here." His eyes continued to scan over her as if he were trying to figure her out. "Your brother was worried about you."

"Oh?" she asked. She'd asked Ben why he'd hired Calvin when she'd had a moment alone with him when Sarah and Lilly had gone inside to take the kids on a bathroom break.

He'd informed her that he'd hired Calvin because he'd needed someone he could trust, and he'd known Calvin longer than anyone else in his life. He trusted the man completely. Besides, he'd been stuck at a dead-end job in the city, or so Ben had told her.

Since they hadn't had a lot of time to chat, Ben had quickly told her that he'd hired him on full time when Lilly had taken off to have her first baby. Then he'd convinced Sarah to hire Calvin permanently when Lilly decided to work from home instead.

"He's struggled with some dark things in his past, and I could hear it in his tone that he needed a fresh start. After Aurora was born, I'd heard that he was looking for work," her brother had told her. "So, when Lilly took off to have Alex, we brought him on. He's been doing great ever since."

"What kind of dark things?" she'd asked, but before her brother could answer, Sarah and the kids had come back.

"You don't really remember me, do you?" Bella asked, turning slightly towards Calvin now. Her eyes had finally adjusted to the bright light, and she was fully awake. The man was sexy, that was for sure. His dark hair was cut short around the sides and left longer on top. He had one of those neatly trimmed beards that she loved on men. But it was his eyes that kept drawing her in and had her trying to avoid them. Somehow, they seemed to almost pierce into her, seeing things she wasn't ready to share with anyone, let alone a stranger.

"Of course, I do." He smiled again, and she felt her heart flutter.

Okay, if she was having a hard time avoiding his eyes, his smile was like the sun. Every single time his lips curved up, showcasing his perfectly pearly whites, her entire body heated.

"Ben was about the only friend I had during a dark time of my life. That summer in Mexico was one of the best of my childhood. I know you may not have seen it as such, but I had needed it." His eyes moved away from hers and he looked off to the horizon.

"It was a good summer," she added quickly. "And now you're working for him?"

"He and Sarah are the best bosses I've had so far," he said with a chuckle.

"My parents wanted to send me to the same boarding school you went to," she admitted, and his eyes returned to hers quickly.

"Oh?" He leaned his elbows on his knees. "What happened?"

She smiled. "Ben saved me." She chuckled. "Well, I ran away first. But in the end, he convinced my parents to allow me to move here." She glanced around again and sighed. "I don't know what I would have done if I hadn't come here." She turned back to him. "They're the ones who allowed me to follow my dreams and sing." She sighed. "Sarah actually was the one who pushed me the most. If it wasn't for her and her mother's connections… I wouldn't have gotten the record deal."

"Crystal is an amazing woman. Her new husband, Rory, is pretty cool too. He's taken over doing all the books for the resort." He chuckled; the deep sound warmed her even more.

"The man saved me on that one since I hate crunching numbers. It freed up my time so I could do more important things."

"Like sitting around the pool, chatting with me?" she joked.

His smile was back. "Yes." He stood up suddenly and straightened his shirt and slacks, a move she'd seen him do earlier. It told her that he was a stickler for perfection. "Well, I'd better get back to work. We have a new group of guests coming in this afternoon. If I can do anything to help make your stay more relaxing, just let me know."

"Thank you." She smiled and watched him walk away. If she'd thought his front side was sexy, watching his butt in the tan slacks as he made his way across the pool deck had her convinced that every part of the man oozed with sex appeal.

When she was alone again, she glanced around. The pool had filled up with more families, and she decided to pack up her things.

The resort had three pool areas, and because she'd been hanging out with her family, they had picked the family-friendly pool to enjoy with the kids. But now, as a large group of parents with young children arrived, she determined she wanted some place quieter to relax. She decided to take a walk instead of heading upstairs, and she strolled through the large gardens until a bead of sweat rolled down between her shoulder blades.

The small private beach area was packed with guests as well. Even the gardens were busy, which had her turning back towards the main building and up the stairs to her room.

After showering and changing into a soft cream sundress, she headed down to the dining room for some dinner. She knew it was early, but her schedule was off, and she figured that the best time to eat was when she was hungry. At least until she acclimated to the time change.

She stepped into the dining hall and was seated by the large windows that overlooked the grounds and the bay outside. The well-maintained yard stretched out to a fence that blocked the cliffs that led down the water's edge on this side of the island. It was one of the best views she'd seen in a while.

She enjoyed the beaches in California, when she'd had a chance to visit them, but watching the waves crash on the rocks below the small cliffs here somehow had her heart filling.

After ordering a glass of wine and a salad with a side of grilled shrimp, she pulled out her phone and looked at the screen for the first time since arriving on the island.

She dreaded knowing if there was anything about the incident circulating in the usual tabloids. After a few clicks, she tossed her phone down and wondered why she'd picked it up in the first place. Of course, there would be outlandish lies spreading. It was Hollywood.

"You okay?" a deep voice asked her.

Glancing up, she smiled at her waiter. "Yes."

"Bad news?" he asked with a slight smile.

"No, just…" She shook her head. "I'm on vacation. I should have known better than to try and look at anything work related." She picked up her wine glass and sipped it as he set her dinner down.

"You don't remember me, do you?" he asked her.

For the first time she ran her eyes over the man. He was tall and thin with jet-black hair and dark deep-set eyes. Not terrible looking, but the fact was, she had no clue if she'd ever met the man before. Had he worked at the resort back when she'd been there before?

"No, sorry." She smiled slightly at him.

Something crossed his eyes, but then he chuckled. "I didn't think so. Ed Simons." He pointed to his chest. "I went to school with you at Brighton."

"Oh." She relaxed slightly and smiled a little more. Even though she didn't remember the guy, she nodded up at him. There were over a hundred kids in her class alone. She'd only known a handful of them when she'd gone to school there. Usually she'd only hung out with her three girlfriends. She hadn't even dated anyone from school back then since she'd struggled with not knowing if her parents would change their minds and show up one day to pull her out of the private school and ship her across the world to a school of their choice.

"You still don't remember me." He frowned slightly.

"I'm sorry." She shook her head. "I didn't have a lot of time to socialize back then."

"No," he agreed. "You kept pretty busy and to yourself. I was valedictorian."

"Of course." She remembered him now. The jet-black hair, the thin frame. He'd changed some in the past few years. His face acne had cleared up and he'd actually gained some weight, even though he was still rail thin. "How are you?"

He rolled his eyes. "Working here." He shrugged. "So much for Harvard or Yale."

"I'm sorry." She frowned.

"Well, we can't all have connections like you, can we?" he added. She was slightly taken aback by his words but guessed that he hadn't meant anything by them. "Let me know if you need anything else," he said, looking over her shoulder.

"Thanks..."

"Ed," he said, not looking down at her before he moved away quickly.

She took one bite of her salad before someone else stopped at her table.

"Evening." Calvin smiled down at her. "Did you enjoy your afternoon?"

She smiled up at him. "Yes." She relaxed and motioned to the chair opposite hers.

"I wish I could," he sighed. "I've got a meeting with the kitchen staff in"—he glanced down at his watch— "five minutes." He sighed. "Gotta get them before the big rush tonight."

"Then I guess it's a good thing I decided to eat dinner early." She smiled and glanced around at the empty dining room. "Best seat in the house, full service, and I only waited about ten minutes for my food."

"Just don't expect that for breakfast, unless you wake up at two in the morning," he joked.

She chuckled. "Until I get used to the time change, I may be waking up at two in the afternoon."

"Either way, we've started serving breakfast all day long." He leaned a little closer to her. "You'd be surprised how many people want pancakes for dinner."

"I've been known to partake in that madness once or twice." She smiled back at him.

His smile doubled. "Let us know if you need anything else. Room service is only a call away. Goodnight." He glanced towards the kitchen doors and started to move away.

"Calvin?" She stopped him before he moved off.

"Yes?" He returned his attention to her.

"I know it's strange of me to ask but, if possible, can I meet with you first thing in the morning?" She'd been thinking about talking to the man about the possibility of an influx of security issues while she was there. Not that she didn't trust the current security measures at the resort. She just wanted to give the man and the employees a heads-up as to what might be coming.

"Sure," he responded easily. "Just let me know once you're up and around. I can make time," he said smoothly.

"Thank you." She relaxed a little.

Instead of moving away, he looked down at her. "Are there problems?"

"No. It's… just precautionary. Thank you."

He nodded again. "Enjoy your dinner." He moved away and she turned back to her meal.

She loved the food from the resort. Adam Carriveau was one of the best chefs around. His food even rivaled the food at some of the Hollywood restaurants she'd enjoyed.

By the time she'd stuffed herself with dinner and had a to-go container filled with cheesecake to take back up to her room, she was wired. But since the sun had set sometime during her dinner and the dining hall had filled with other guests, she decided to spend the rest of her evening upstairs, alone.

She had planned on spending part of this trip writing and working on a few new songs she had in mind. And she figured the best time to work on them was when she was in self-quarantine. After all, there was nothing else she could do while she waited for her world to settle back down and return to normal. If it ever did.

CHAPTER FOUR

*C*alvin didn't really mind the crazy hours of his job at the resort. He normally clocked out shortly before the dinner rush most days and was on shift an hour before the breakfast rush.

There were exceptions to that, however, and last night had been one. With the large party that had come in for a family reunion, he'd been forced to oversee room changes, party details, and a few disgruntled employees who had argued over shift changes. He'd finally gotten home around ten last night and had arrived back on the island around five that morning. He knew that today was going to be another long day, since the first formal party for the Schaffer group was that afternoon and he was on schedule to oversee that everything ran smoothly.

Heather, the resort's official events director, oversaw all the details, but it was his job to ensure that all the employees were in place to fill each task.

It was like a dance each morning as the employees moved around getting ready for the breakfast rush.

He didn't expect to see most of the guests downstairs

searching for food until after eight, though there were the occasional early risers, mostly older people or parents with younger kids.

He hadn't expected to see Bella until sometime after noon and was surprised when he stepped into the dining hall to see her sipping a cup of coffee and looking out over the lawn.

Her long locks were piled on top of her head in a messy bun, and she had a large hoodie on that engulfed her, making her appear smaller and frail. Her legs were tucked up under her as she stared out over the water. She looked deep in thought, and he was about to head down to the kitchen to make sure everything was running smoothly when she glanced over and waved him over to her.

"Good morning." He smiled down at her.

"Morning." She motioned for him to sit. "Do you have time?"

"Sure." He sat down and waited as Heather, one of the waitstaff, delivered Bella's breakfast.

"Morning, boss man." Heather smiled at him. "Want a cup of joe?"

He nodded. "Thanks, Heather." The teenager moved away and came back less than a minute later to pour a cup for him. "If you need anything else," she said smoothly to Bella.

"Thank you." Bella smiled up at the girl.

"How did you sleep?" he asked, once they were alone.

"Wonderfully." She smiled and took a deep breath. "I'd forgotten how fresh the air is here and how it helps me sleep." She took a bite of her breakfast, which he noted was a small bowl of fruit yogurt and a piece of raisin bread on the side. She looked unsatisfied with the simple meal. "You?"

"Yes," he answered and waited for her to open up to him about what was bothering her. He could see something deep behind her eyes. Even though she looked refreshed, there was something eating at her.

When she set her spoon down and took a sip of her coffee, he could see the decision to share with him cross her eyes.

"I don't know if you read the tabloid papers…" she started, avoiding his eyes. He didn't respond to her, and she looked up, her dark eyes meeting his.

"No," he finally answered. "I don't fall into the gossip trap."

She nodded quickly. "Then I'll start at the beginning." She leaned back slightly. "I'm having issues with… a man."

"Okay," he said when she didn't continue.

"One that has power." She closed her eyes. "Have you heard of Michael Himes?"

He was silent for a moment. "The director?"

She nodded slowly. "We… went out on a few arranged dates."

"Isn't he like… twenty years older than you?"

She shook her head. "That's your takeaway from this?"

He shrugged. "Sorry. Continue."

"Anyway, after the second date, I saw him for the man he was, and I stopped taking his calls and text messages."

"What happened next?" he asked, taking another sip of his coffee.

"He continued calling. So, I decided to meet him and officially break things off. Face to face."

"He didn't go for it?" he asked, searching her face. He could see the answer before she even opened her mouth.

"No." She sighed. "If anything, the meeting made things worse."

"How so?" he asked, growing more concerned.

"He… started showing up everywhere I was."

"Stalking you?" He felt his temper for the man and his concern for Bella grow.

Instead of answering, she nodded and reached for her mug.

He took a couple of cleansing breaths. "Then I guess it's a good thing you left California."

She avoided his eyes again, and he could tell there was more to the story.

"Did anything else happen?" he asked after a moment of silence.

"No." She shook her head and avoided his eyes. He wanted to ask her to tell him more, but he didn't want to come across as pushy. "I just needed… time away from everything." She glanced out the window again. "It looks like you're setting up for a big party."

He followed her gaze and saw the large circular tables being rolled out to the lawn and set up for the family reunion lunch.

"Yes," he answered, knowing she was changing the subject but figuring he'd allow it for now. "There's a big family reunion today. They'll have lunch out on the lawn and have booked the bigger pool area for a private dinner." He thought of all the things that still needed to be done to prepare the space.

"I'm keeping you," she said, interrupting his thoughts.

"No," he lied. The truth was, he could happily spend the entire morning sitting there talking with her. That thought had him standing up quickly. "But I will leave you to enjoy the rest of your breakfast." He picked up his coffee mug but leaned down closer to her before he walked away to add, "You know, Adam's French Toast Fosters is the best in Maine." He chuckled when her eyes heated at the thought of something better than simple yogurt.

He took his coffee down to the kitchen for his morning meeting with Adam and his staff and wasn't surprised when an order for French Toast Fosters came in a few moments later.

After getting the following week's orders from Adam, he headed back up to his office on the top floor. Sarah and Ben kept the big office just down the hall but, shortly after they had hired him on, they had renovated a room down the hall from their office into an office space for him.

For the next few hours, he busied himself sending out the orders for the kitchens and the bars. By the time lunch rolled around, he had most of his office work done. He made his way out to the employees' patio bar and sat outside and enjoyed his lunch with the rest of the employees on their breaks.

The sun was high overhead but the thick leaves from the large maple trees shaded the picnic benches that had been set up for the employees.

It was days like this that reminded him why he loved where he worked. The sunbeams caused the blue water to sparkle. It's soothing motion and the sound of it lapping at the rocky shore was the best music to his ears. Any time he needed to meditate, he thought of this place. Of moments like this.

He watched as the ferry dropped off a few guests and took a small group to the mainland for a day trip to the shops. The nearby town of Silver Cove, with its historic main street and quaint little shops, was another big draw.

He wasn't surprised to see JT at the helm. He knew his wife Emma and the kids had a standard nap time just after lunch.

That got Calvin thinking about kids. With those thoughts, he was forced to try and clear his mind to shake off the bad mood that always came when he thought of what he'd lost.

As always, the memory of Kelly only brought him pain. He tried to fight the dark thoughts back as much as he could, since he knew that it would take him hours to get rid of the funk.

He needed to check on the lunch party, so he finished his sandwich and strolled the grounds.

Before he came to the opening, he almost bumped into Bella, who was rushing towards the dock with fear in her eyes. The look on her face had him holding onto her shoulders and glancing around.

"What's wrong?" he asked quickly.

"Cal…" She shook her head and, after a moment, closed her eyes as she took several deep breaths. "I… um, got a call." When she opened her eyes, most of the fear was gone. "I'm sorry, I had a phone call that spooked me."

He took her shoulders and moved them to a small private bench surrounded by bushes filled with brightly colored flowers.

She sat next to him and composed herself. It took her several deep breaths before her breathing leveled off.

"You okay?" he asked.

Her dark eyes moved to him. "Yes. I guess I let the call affect me more than I should have." She tried to smile at him.

"Want to tell me what the caller said?"

Again, her eyes moved around as if she was looking for something or someone to jump out at her.

"No. It's probably nothing. I'm just overreacting."

"Are you sure?" He took her hand in his. It was small and soft, and he felt her relax even more as he held it.

"It's just… someone keeps calling me and… saying things. Terrible things."

"Like?" He stopped her before she could answer. "No, sorry, don't answer that. Why does it scare you?"

She closed her eyes again. "Because the things that he says… it's horrible. He talks about mutilating me."

His hands jerked in hers and tightened, then he took a

few breaths and relaxed.

"Have you thought about changing your number?" he asked.

"I have, twice now."

"You're sure the caller is a he?" he asked. She turned to him and nodded. "Could it be Himes?"

She shrugged her shoulders. "I just don't know. It would make sense. He's the only one who's been… strange."

"You said he was following you?"

"I'm not sure if you can officially call it following." She bit her bottom lip. The slight move had his desire for her growing as images of kissing those lips surfaced.

Shifting his mind, he asked, "Why don't you start at the beginning?" But before she could say anything, his phone went off.

Seeing the front desk's number, he cringed. "Sorry, I have to…"

She nodded and he answered.

"Calvin here." He listened to Stacey explain how the cake for the main event tonight had gone missing in the kitchen and that they needed him to help find it and to explain to the Schaffers that their cake was MIA.

After hanging up, he turned to Bella. "I'm sorry. Raincheck?" he asked her.

"Yes." She smiled and started getting up. He took her elbow in his hands and helped her up.

"How about after dinner?" he asked. "I can meet you?" He glanced around. "How about at the gazebo?" She was silent for a moment, thinking. "I'd like to help you. If you're going to be staying here, under our protection, maybe it would help if I knew the entire story?" He tilted his head. "Or I could call your brother…"

"No." She shook her head quickly. "Eight o'clock. The gazebo," she agreed. Then she walked away quickly.

CHAPTER FIVE

ella had only agreed to meet Calvin later that evening because of the look in his eyes when she'd been talking to him. The look of pure concern couldn't be faked. That and, well, she'd been really spooked about the call.

She'd had several since she'd broken things off with Michael. They'd gotten darker each time.

It was true, she'd changed her cell number a few times now, each time only giving it out to family and Maggie, her agent.

She knew she could trust Calvin since her brother and Sarah trusted the man to run the resort. There was also the fact that she'd had a major crush on him all those years ago.

In the past few years, almost everyone she ran into would recognize her, and their eyes would grow large. She could tell right away that they were starstruck. Calvin didn't act that way around her and it was so refreshing.

Calvin didn't show any signs of caring who she was even though she'd seen the spark of attraction behind his dark eyes. Attraction that probably matched that in her own eyes.

She spent the rest of her day up in her room, strumming her guitar as she worked on a few new songs. She tried to get the deep voice out of her head, but the stress reflected in the music she played.

Finally, she gave up and turned on the television to watch an old sitcom so she could laugh instead of worry.

She had dinner delivered to her room. She didn't want to deal with anyone else at the moment. After eating, she felt much better and picked up the guitar again. When she was in the mood to play, she liked as few distractions as possible.

She'd set an alarm so she wouldn't work past the time to meet Calvin and had given it a lot of thought as to what she was going to tell him and what she wasn't.

As she walked down the stairs, out the front lobby area, and down the dark pathway, she tried to settle her nerves. She didn't know if she was more anxious about seeing Calvin or telling him everything that had been going on with her over the past few months.

The moment she stepped outside, she realized she should have looked out the window before heading out. The warm sunny day had turned misty and cooler, making her wish she had grabbed a light jacket. She stepped up her pace and, by the time she made it to the gazebo, she was warmer.

Calvin was there, leaning against the railing, looking out over the dark water. When he heard her approach, he turned and smiled at her and her steps faltered.

There were strings of white lights hanging from the eves of the small circular covering, which highlighted the brightness of the man's smile.

He was still wearing dark gray dress pants and a crisp white button-up shirt, but he'd removed the tie he'd worn earlier and had rolled up the sleeves of the shirt. He looked even sexier than when he'd sat with her during breakfast.

"Did you enjoy your breakfast?" he asked smoothly with a

smile that told her he knew full well that she'd taken his advice and ordered the French toast.

"I did," she answered, stopping directly beside him. "Then again, I don't think I've ever had anything bad come from the kitchen here."

He nodded in agreement. "Want to sit?" He motioned to the bench. When she sat down, he frowned over at her. "You should have worn a jacket." He picked up his jacket, which he'd tossed over the railing, and gently placed it over her shoulders.

"Thank you." She sighed and enjoyed the instant warmth and the sexy male scent that surrounded her. "I didn't look outside before heading down."

He waited, watching her. "Busy day?"

She smiled. "I finished working on a couple of new songs." She felt the flood of accomplishment that always followed the completion of a song.

"Wow, good." He tilted his head slightly. "I've always wondered what the process was." He moved slightly until his eyes met hers. "I mean, do you play while writing or write, then create the notes to match?"

She shrugged. "For me, I strum the guitar and the lyrics just come to me. Sometimes," she admitted.

She could tell he was skirting around the subject and decided to jump right in.

"I mentioned Michael." She took a deep breath. "That I'd gone out on a few dates with him. Well, those dates were more like... promotional opportunities. At least I thought they were." She remembered the excitement when Maggie had told her about the deal she'd made.

Bella's song "Someday Hope" had been selected as the main tune in the soundtrack for Michael's latest movie, *Rivers Crossing*.

Maggie had arranged for Bella to attend the premiere

with the director. She'd been so excited meeting and being around all the big-name stars that she'd allowed the bright lights and stars to blind her for the entire night. She'd overlooked the man's obvious faults.

When he'd called her directly and asked her to attend another event with him, she'd jumped at the chance.

Naturally, pictures of them from the events had been plastered everywhere. She couldn't go to a checkout counter without seeing her and Michael's faces along with headlines that hinted at how far their relationship had come in such a short time.

By the second date, the bright lights and blinders she'd worn were quickly fading. They'd been removed completely that last night when he'd driven her home himself.

She'd made it clear to him that she had an early morning recording session and needed to get home so she could get plenty of rest. But instead of heading towards her apartment downtown, he'd turned onto the highway and started heading towards the Hollywood hills.

"What happened?" Calvin asked, and she realized she hadn't stopped talking.

Her eyes moved up to his instead of her fingers, which she'd been staring at while she'd told him everything.

Swallowing, she continued.

"He pulled up in front of his house, one of those massive mansions that hangs on the side of the hills overlooking the city." She remembered feeling helpless and cornered. "He talked me into going inside and tried to convince me…"

Calvin shifted and broke her attention. Shaking her head, she sighed.

"I didn't sleep with him. At first, I thought I wanted to, but then, he… changed." She shook her head, unable to explain exactly what she'd witnessed.

"How so?"

"It's hard to explain, but he turned… scary." She held in a shiver as she wrapped her arms around her, pulling his jacket closer to her for warmth.

"What happened next?" he asked softly.

She took a deep breath. "I… stood my ground, and shot off a text to my agent, who had an Uber driver pulling up out front less than five minutes later with instructions to not let off the doorbell until I came outside." She smiled. "Maggie is pretty protective."

"Something tells me that wasn't the last of it." He almost groaned it out.

"That was the last time I was with Michael alone." She leaned back in the bench and glanced out across the darkness of the water. The lights from the resort were gleaming behind them, casting shadows across the lawn from the trees. She could hear the water below lapping at the rocks that lined the jagged shore of the island.

"You said he was stalking you?" he asked after a moment of silence.

"After that, it seemed that he was everywhere I was." She glanced over at him and, with his face masked in shadows, she realized he was even more handsome than she'd first believed.

She thought about telling him about the dark notes, the threatening emails, and that last scary night outside the club when she'd bumped into him, but she held in the rest as he looked thoughtfully at her.

"Did you file a restraining order?" he asked.

She shook her head slowly. "My agent thought…" The look he gave her had her shutting her mouth.

"You should have," he said softly.

"There wasn't really any reason to. I mean, there was no proof that he was officially stalking me. After all, I was in very public places and we were both still promoting…" She shrugged remembering running into Michael at her local grocery store. Since she knew exactly where he lived, she doubted it was just coincidence that they'd bumped into one another. "Besides, it was his word against mine." She frowned down at her hands and realized that she was picking at her nails again and tucked them into the deep pockets of his jacket. "So, do you like working at the resort?"

He chuckled. "Time to change subjects?"

She took a deep breath. "I did come here to get away from all my problems."

He nodded. "One last thing, then I'll grace you with my entire backstory." His smile slipped slightly. "Is he the only one you're worried about?"

She shifted under his gaze as she nodded. "He's the only one I know about, yes."

His eyes narrowed slightly, and he picked up her hands and held them lightly. "While you're here, let me assure you that I will personally make sure that you are safe."

"Thank you." Bella relaxed slightly.

He nodded, looking slightly uncomfortable, then his grin was back. "Now, what do you want to know about me?"

She chuckled and thought about all the questions she had for him. What had he been up to after school? Was he in a relationship?

She'd been so young when her parents had shipped Ben off to boarding school. By the time she and Ben had gotten to spend time together, real time, he'd already been with Sarah.

"What was my brother like as a teenager?" She leaned her elbow on the back of the chair and waited for him to answer. "I mean, we always took family vacations together, but…" She shrugged.

Watching him chuckle, she couldn't help but smile.

"Don't hold back on me either. Every time Ben would

come home for the holidays, he'd tell me all sorts of crazy stories about the two of you. All the trouble you'd get into."

His smile slipped and, suddenly, a sad distant look crossed his eyes, making them grow darker. Instantly, she wanted to know what had caused the sadness, but she knew that he would hold some things back just as she had done to him.

CHAPTER SIX

After spending an hour talking with Bella, he felt like he knew more about her and her brother's relationship. He knew that Bella had been very young when their parents had shipped Ben off to school.

Ben had never held anything back about where he'd come from, who his family was, and how his parents had treated them.

Then there had been that summer he'd gone to Mexico with their family. It was either that or be stuck at the school all summer, alone. Thankfully, Ben had talked his parents into letting him tag along, and he'd convinced his parents to give him the money to do so.

After all, they hadn't wanted to see him. Not after what he'd done.

The more Bella talked about her and her brother's relationship, the harder it was keeping his emotions in check. He had to consciously make sure that his face was blank every time she mentioned how her brother had saved her from a life dominated by her parents.

So many thoughts of how he could have done things differently in his youth rushed through his mind as she told her stories.

By the time he finally stepped into his house on the mainland, it was just past midnight. He wasn't scheduled to work the following day but had mentioned that he'd be available if she needed anything. He'd even given her his private phone number for emergencies, something he never would have done for any other guest at the resort.

He'd purchased his four-story gray Victorian cottage, which sat on its own little private bluff, shortly after getting the job at the resort. The place had needed some work when he'd moved in, but Ben had been eager to help out, along with Sarah's cousin, Rowan.

He had believed that the four-bedroom cottage that overlooked a small private rocky beach was perfect, but lately, he'd realized just how lonely he was in the place. Especially when he returned home to the dark place. He'd thought about getting a dog like most of his friends had, but then he realized the thing would be locked away all day alone. He just couldn't do that to an animal.

After tossing down his jacket, the one he'd lent Bella earlier, he knew that with all the memories that had surfaced again, it would be hours before he could fall asleep. So, instead, he changed into some gym shorts and an old T-shirt, made his way down to his basement, and spent an hour lifting weights.

After showering off the sweat, he was still wired, so he pulled open his laptop.

The first thing that came to his mind was checking up on Michael Himes. The man was one of the most powerful directors in Hollywood. He had almost half a dozen hits under his belt and, according to several websites, had a net worth of several hundred million.

There were hundreds of pictures of the man, each one with a different beautiful woman on his arm. The top dozen or so pictures were of Bella and the guy. Most of the images were of the same night from different angles. Some had even been photoshopped to change the color of Bella's dress or to add brighter lighting. Someone had even photoshopped the couple onto a beach somewhere with a headline above them that read "Bella and Michael Elope."

He read several articles about the pair and even watched a few YouTube clips of them answering questions at what he supposed was their first arranged date.

Bella looked nervous but beautiful in a shiny teal dress that clung to her like a second skin. The diamonds in her ears sparkled in the spotlight as she talked about her new album.

Suddenly, he realized that he had yet to hear her sing. Sure, he knew that she was extremely popular and had just wrapped up her second album, but he didn't really get a lot of time to listen to the radio.

Changing gears, he clicked on one of her music videos and, after "Someday Hope" started playing, he felt his heart flip in his chest. The video was filled with scenes from the movie *River Crossing*, but she did make a few appearances sitting along the beach and strumming a guitar by a campfire.

Leaning back, he watched the next video. It was a black-and-white music video of her playing the piano in a field of barley as she sang the sad words to her next song, "Take Me Back." He wondered instantly who she'd written the song for? Was it an old lover?

More than an hour later, he crawled into his bed with the memory of the sweet voice replaying in his head.

He woke several hours later to the sound of his cell phone

ringing. Opening one eye, he glanced at the screen and moaned.

"This better be important," he told Ben.

Hearing Ben's chuckle, he laid his head back on the pillow.

"Not important, but it could be fun," Ben answered.

He groaned and glanced at his clock. It was a quarter past eight.

"It's my day off."

"Yeah, but we need another body and your boat," Ben said. "Besides, Bella said that she enjoyed hanging out with you last night."

At the mention of Bella, his eyes flew open. "She did?" He instantly regretted sounding like a high schooler.

When Ben chuckled, he knew his friend thought the same.

"What are you? Fifteen?" Ben laughed. "Get dressed, we'll be there in ten to pick you up."

"For?" he asked, swinging his legs off the bed.

"We're taking your boat out. Crystal has the kids for the day. We need some adult time on the water," Ben said. "Now it's nine minutes."

"Jesus." Calvin groaned as he stood up and wiped his free hand over his face.

Ben laughed and hung up.

Exactly nine minutes later, he was opening the door for the group.

Ben, Sarah, Rowan, Kayla, and even Adam and Lilly strolled into his house like they owned the place. Bella was the only one who didn't walk in. Everyone was comfortable around his place. They had been there enough to know to make themselves at home. He felt the same around their homes, since the group often hung out together.

Rowan even walked over to the fridge and glanced in.

"Told you he'd have some beer in here." He glanced over at him. "Mind if we pack it up?"

"Go ahead." He glanced around towards Bella. "Please." He motioned for her to enter, since she was still standing just outside his front door. "Come on in."

She was wearing a pair of cream-colored shorts and a soft blue tank top. She'd tied her long hair over to the side in a loose braid.

"Sorry about this." She shrugged as she glanced around his entryway. "I kept telling my brother that I would be fine as a seventh wheel, but he insisted." She sighed. "We need an even eight." She waved her hands and mimicked her brother's tone.

He smiled. "It's okay. I can't tell you how many times this has happened to me."

"Where's your cooler?" Ben called to him from his mudroom. "The big one?"

Calvin chuckled and then called out. "It's in the garage."

Ben disappeared into the mudroom that led to the garage and came back with the cooler and a case of beer he'd stored in the garage. "I'll pay you back for these. We forgot to hit the liquor store."

"Have you eaten?" Sarah asked him.

"Not yet."

"You look like we woke you," Bella added.

He chuckled. "Ben did and I bet he doesn't feel an ounce of sorrow for the act."

"None whatsoever," Ben called out as he dumped all the ice from his freezer into the cooler and then started adding the beer.

"Score," Rowan added pulling out a bag of chips and tucking them under his arm.

"I've packed enough food for all of us," Adam mentioned.

"Yeah, no matter how good your fancy snacks are, they can't beat potato chips," Rowan answered.

"Heathen," Adam joked.

"I like your house," Bella said, still standing by him.

"Thanks." He smiled. "Your brother and Rowan helped fix the place up a couple of years back." He glanced around and was thankful that he paid Sandra, one of the housekeeping employees, to clean the place once a week for him. It was out of necessity, since he spent most of his days on the island dealing with resort issues.

"You ready?" Ben asked when the cooler was loaded.

"Sure." He grabbed his jacket from the hook by the door.

They all piled into Rowan's truck and Ben's SUV. Calvin sat in the very back of the SUV with Bella beside him.

"How often does this happen?" she asked as they made their way towards the docks.

He thought about it. "Once a month in the warmer months and at least once in the winter." He shrugged. "It's kind of our thing." He relaxed back and realized that he could use a day out on the water with his friends.

"Do they ever plan it?" Bella asked.

He laughed.

"What's so funny?" Ben called back to him.

"Your sister is under the impression that you plan things."

The entire car burst out laughing.

"He used to," Sarah called back to them. "But then we had kids and well... Anything that has to do with our private lives is more on-the-fly style."

Bella shook her head. "But they run the business and the kids..."

He smiled over at her. "That's different. When Crystal says she's going to take the kids for the day, they jump and scramble to arrange this." He motioned to the group as the SUV parked at the docks. "I've just learned to go with it and enjoy. Thankfully, I was already scheduled off for the day. Several times they've actually pulled me away from work."

Bella smiled as he helped her out of the back of the car. "Nothing like having a friend for a boss, huh?"

He nodded towards the large sailboat and the group of friends loading supplies in it and smiled. "It has its perks."

CHAPTER SEVEN

She'd been on plenty of boats in her life. After all, when she'd lived with Ben and Sarah, they'd taken her out several times. Not even the ferry rides back and forth to the resort had ever scared her. But looking up at the tall mast as she stood at the end of the dock while everyone loaded up the day's supplies, she started second-guessing herself.

"You okay?" Calvin stopped beside her. His hands were full of fishing poles.

"Yes," she lied easily.

He chuckled and handed the poles to Rowan, then turned towards her and took her shoulders into his hands. "You look a little green and we haven't even stepped off the dock yet."

She took a deep breath, sucking in the taste of the saltwater and the cool breeze floating in off the water, trying to calm herself down. "I just…" She shook her head. "I've never been on a sailboat this big before."

He glanced up at the sail and then turned back to her. "It's just like any other boat. We only put up the sail if the winds are good. Other than that"—he turned her slightly and pointed her in the direction of the back of the boat— "it's got a motor we use."

She relaxed slightly, glancing up at the sail again. "I'm not sure why I'm nervous," she admitted, feeling stupid. When he held out his hand for hers, she took another deep breath and set hers in it and allowed him to pull her easily onto the boat, lifting her slightly.

For a split second, she felt weightless and free. The feeling was intoxicating, and she allowed herself to be shuffled to a long flat section under the sail.

"Sit here," he said, motioning to the area. "This way you'll be out of the way and still have the best view."

"Everything okay?" Sarah stopped beside them.

"Yes," Calvin answered automatically. "Just showing Bella the ropes." He smiled back at Sarah.

"Cool," Sarah answered, shifting a bag. "We'll be ready to push off in a few minutes." She disappeared down a narrow set of steps.

"I'm going to go help out. Will you be okay?" he asked her softly.

Since she didn't trust her voice not to shake, she nodded and quickly sat down. She felt better when she wrapped her fingers around a thick rope dangling in front of her.

She watched as everyone else moved around, preparing the boat for their day trip. She was so occupied watching Calvin that she hadn't noticed they'd left the dock. Her fingers tightened on the rope until Calvin moved in front of her and bent down until they were eye to eye.

"Hey." He touched her knee gently with his hands. "Are you doing okay?"

"Yes," she lied again.

He chuckled. "You are a terrible liar." His hands reached for hers and started rubbing them slowly. "You've been on boats before, yes?"

"Yes," she admitted and nodded.

"Then you've got this." He smiled up at her and her eyes locked with his. She noticed how much lighter they were than her own. Where she had dark eyes the color of coffee, his were more caramel colored.

Then she looked down at their joined hands and a thought of how his would feel roaming over her flashed in her mind. Would they be soft? Rough? Something told her that he would know just what to do to please her. She doubted he would fumble around like Sam, her first, had.

His hands shook hers, and she realized he was talking, and she hadn't heard a word he'd said.

"Sorry," she replied.

His chuckle warmed her. "It's okay." His thumb was tracing the inside of her palm, moving up to her wrist and continuing moving in slow circles. "You know, we're not going too far from the shore." He nodded towards the rocky cliffs just off the side of the boat.

"That's not it." She glanced up tentatively then her eyes grew as the boat bobbed slightly.

"Is it the sail?" he asked.

She shook her head. "I... don't know. I guess it's the thought of not being in control."

"Okay, come with me." He stood up and reached out his hand for hers.

She shook her head quickly and tightened her grip on the rope.

He leaned closer and lowered his voice until he was almost whispering. "Trust me."

There was something in his dark eyes that told her she could trust him, something almost mesmerizing, so she reached out her hand as she held her breath.

He wrapped an arm around her waist as they made their way back to where Adam was standing behind the wheel. Her brother and Rowan were sitting nearby getting the fishing poles ready. The women were laying blankets out to sunbathe on.

"Think we can take over for a while?" Calvin asked easily.

Adam shrugged and stepped aside. "She is all yours," he said in his deep French accent.

Calvin smiled at her. "Come here." He nudged her until she stood between him and the large wooden wheel.

He took her hands and placed them on the wheel, keeping his bigger hands over hers as they steered the sailboat across the water.

She relaxed slightly when her back bumped into his front. Just feeling his strong arms around her, holding her as she took control of the boat, had her letting a deep breath of relief out.

"Better?" he asked, his breath so close to her ear that it caused small bumps to rise over her skin.

She closed her eyes and tried to stop herself from moaning with want. Nodding, she relaxed a little more.

"Think you can enjoy yourself now?" he asked softly, nudging her hands slightly so that the boat turned a little, lining them up with the shore.

"I… guess so."

"Hey, sis," Ben called out, and she and Calvin both turned towards him as he snapped a picture of them. Laughing, his brother looked at his screen. "At least you're not as green as you were before," Ben added.

"Jackass," she said to her brother and instantly felt better as anger took over. Ben snapped another picture of them, then laughed.

"You still love me," Ben called back as he wrapped an arm around Sarah, who playfully slapped his shoulder and hugged him back. "Sarah used to get sick when I'd take her out when she was pregnant."

"Did you stop taking her out?" Bella asked him.

"No," Sarah answered. "He just learned that if I was pissed at him, I couldn't focus on being sick." She shifted so she could see Bella more clearly. "It worked." She smiled.

"Okay." She took a deep breath. "I could be pissed at him." She nodded then glanced back towards Calvin, and her anger for her brother fell away as desire for Calvin took over. Having him so close to her had caused her body to almost vibrate.

After a moment, she realized that when she'd been imagining what it would be like to be with Calvin, she hadn't been focused on her fears.

As the boat carried them further away from the dock, she dreamed about Calvin's hands on her as his body lightly bumped up against her own.

When she heard the motor cut off, she glanced around. Calvin had reached over and cut the engine without stepping away from her.

"We're here," he said with a smile and, for a split second, she marveled at the feeling of his chest against her shoulders. Then he stepped back, leaving her swaying slightly as she still gripped the wheel lightly.

The boat was bobbing in the middle of a small cove.

"This is the perfect spot," Adam said, tossing an anchor into the water. It caught and the boat jerked to a halt.

"Think you can come up front with the rest of us?" he asked her.

She nodded and followed him around the deck. She made her way around the other couples as the men all finished getting the fishing poles ready while Sarah, Lilly, and Kayla chatted as they tanned themselves on the deck.

"Doing okay?" Calvin asked.

"Yes, thank you. I feel so stupid."

"Fear is nothing to feel bad about." He leaned closer to her. "I'm afraid of heights myself."

"You are?" As an answer, he nodded. Then he smiled and glanced over her shoulder. "Look, dolphins." He pointed.

She turned quickly and watched as a fin disappeared less than twenty feet from the hull of the boat.

By the time Adam pulled out the lunch he'd packed for the group that morning, she had all but forgotten her fear of being on the sailboat.

It wasn't rational, the fear. She couldn't explain what had come over her, but just seeing the tall mast sway had her knees going weak.

The men chose one side of the hull to fish off while the women took the other. There were friendly wagers about who would catch the largest or the most fish.

They all took a break and sat around eating the picnic. Even though the guys had to sit directly on the deck, dangling their feet overboard while the women sat on top of the cabin, she had to admit that it was one of the best picnics she'd had in a long time.

The view was the best, the company was even better, and the food was off the charts. Not to mention Calvin sat at her feet cracking jokes back and forth with the rest of the guys, which had her entertained all through lunch.

Sarah, Kayla, Lilly, and Bella all decided after lunch to sunbathe on the deck instead of fish. Stripping off her tank top and shorts, she laid out on the cushions they had spread out on the top of the cabin.

Lying in the sun with her friends as she sipped a cold beer someone had handed her, she felt herself slowly returning to normal.

She had even started to fall asleep but then she heard another boat engine, and her brother cursed under his breath.

Looking up, she saw a small speedboat quickly approach them.

"What the…" Ben barked out as the boat came dangerously close to them, causing the sailboat to bob in the other boat's wake. Then he handed his fishing pole to Adam. Bella was shocked when the man on the deck pulled out a camera and started snapping pictures.

"What's going…" Sarah asked as she sat up and glanced around. Then she turned to Bella. "Cover up." Her sister-in-law threw a towel towards her. "Get below deck."

She didn't get the chance to do anything, since Calvin was there, wrapping the large towel around her and pulling her down the narrow stairs.

When they were below deck, she had to blink a few times for her eyes to adjust. Tears stung her eyes as she tried to control her anger and emotions.

"How did they find me?" she groaned out.

"Who knows, but until they're gone, we're staying put."

She hadn't gone below deck before. It was bigger than she'd imagined it would be.

When her eyes adjusted, she realized he was still holding the large towel around her bikini-clad body. He'd removed his T-shirt sometime after lunch when he'd been fishing. She'd dreamed of what he'd look like without a shirt, but still the perfect muscles that stretched over him were mouth-watering.

"Thank you." She took the towel from him and moved over to sit on the sofa area by the small kitchen area. A queen-sized bed was shoved to the front of the cabin.

"Stay put. We'll let you know when it's clear," Sarah called down to them as she poked her head in the doorway and then shut the small door quickly before they had time to respond. With the door shut, they were bathed in full darkness.

Calvin moved over and sat beside her as she tied the towel around her body.

She leaned back and realized that she was still a little groggy from being woken from her nap.

"Hey." He wrapped his arm around her shoulder. "I'm sure your brother can handle getting rid of them."

"Oh, I'm sure he can. If he can't, Sarah will."

Calvin chuckled. The rich deep sound of it made her body vibrate and her eyes snake down to his lips then slowly over his chest.

She'd dreamed about how his lips would feel over her own. Over her skin. Her fingers itched to touch him, to explore his tanned, toned body.

"Did you get some sleep?" he asked her.

"Hm," she said, licking her lips. If she tried hard enough, she could just imagine what he'd taste like.

Since they could still hear the other boat motor outside, circling them, she knew it would probably take an act of god or the police to get rid of the paparazzi.

"I think there's a third boat." Calvin moved closer to her and she held her breath as his bare skin moved inches from her own. Then she realized he was looking out a small porthole behind her head.

"Yeah." He sighed. "There's two more."

They felt their own boat start to move. "Looks like we're making a run for it," he added. She closed her eyes and leaned back.

He touched her shoulder. "You okay?"

She didn't open her eyes as she nodded. She didn't mind being up on the deck when they'd moved, but now, feeling the rocking of the boat down here where there wasn't any fresh air… she felt her stomach roll.

Then she felt Calvin's fingers on her face. She opened her

eyes as he brushed a strand of hair that had come loose from her braid away from her face.

"Need something to take your mind off it?" he asked softly. His eyes moved to her lips for a split second.

"Calvin," she sighed, and pulled his face to hers. The kiss was light as she splayed her fingers in his hair, holding him to her.

The distraction worked perfectly. Instead of feeling the sway of the boat as they moved, all she could feel was her body tremble with want. At first, he'd stilled, as if he hadn't expected the kiss, but then when she'd moaned and brushed her tongue against his lips, he'd moved.

Pushing her back against the cushions, he deepened the kiss, tasting her. She opened for him, needing more, wanting… everything.

The towel she'd wrapped around her body fell away leaving them skin to skin. Her hands moved over his arms, his shoulders, needing to explore him. She marveled at the feeling of his hard body over hers.

Slowly, his fingers left her face, brushing lightly down her neck, until they rested on her shoulders.

"Bella," he said between kisses.

"Please," she begged, "help me." She didn't quite know what she was asking. All she knew was that she didn't want him to stop.

His hands brushed further down her body as his mouth came back to hers. When he cupped her breast, she arched into his palm and groaned as he nudged the triangle of her swimsuit top aside and ran her erect nipple between his fingers.

She felt herself grow wet. It had been too long since she'd felt this much want.

He dipped his head down, and she moaned softly as his

mouth covered her nipple. He took it into his mouth and sucked lightly. Her entire body felt on the verge of exploding.

Then the engine to the boat died and he jerked back. His eyes ran over her quickly before he reached up and covered her breast with her suit. She had a moment to recover as he stood up just as the door was yanked open.

"The cops are here," Lilly called down to them. "Stay put. We're explaining what's going on. The idiots are going to kill someone driving like that. I doubt they're going to stick around much longer. But we've decided to head in for the day." She glanced at Bella. "You doing okay?" she asked her.

"Yes." Bella was shocked she'd found her voice to answer.

Lilly's eyes moved back to Calvin and suddenly she smiled. "Okay." She shut the door again.

"She knows." Bella sighed and leaned back.

"What?" Calvin's voice rose slightly, causing Bella to chuckle.

"Take it easy. It's not a crime." She looked up at him. He ran his hands through his hair, causing it to stand up a little more. It had been standing up since she'd run her fingers through his dark locks moments before.

"Bella, listen," he started, his eyes going everywhere but her own.

She chuckled as she stood up quickly. "Don't sweat it. I get it." She nodded, trying to swallow the pain.

CHAPTER EIGHT

*H*ow could she understand why he was struggling with kissing her? Ben was his best friend. He'd do anything for the guy. There were plenty of rules about bros before hoes… he glanced over to where Bella sat on the sofa. She hadn't wrapped the towel around her again, leaving her clad only in the small material of her bikini. Material he'd pulled aside to enjoy… Shit. He sighed and cleared his mind of what he'd just enjoyed.

"It's just…" He glanced towards the door, trying to get the taste and the wonderful feeling of Bella out of his mind. "Ben. He's… my best friend."

"And," she started as she stood up. He watched her sway slightly as the boat moved. "I'm his little sister," she said, sounding annoyed.

"Yes," Calvin said, relieved that she was starting to understand.

Then the boat shuttered as a wave hit them, and she started to pitch. Reaching up, he wrapped his arms around her waist to steady her.

His eyes locked with hers as her hands moved up to his

shoulders. Instantly, the memory of the taste of her almost overwhelmed him. Her soft body was pressed up against his.

"This won't end well," he said softly as he looked down at her.

"No reason not to have some fun." She licked her lips again. The simple move was more erotic than anything he'd ever seen before.

"There are plenty of reasons." He tried to hold himself steady by thinking of her request to keep her safe while she was there.

"Cal," she started, but then the boat started moving again. He had to reach up to steady them both.

"You'd better sit back down," he said. "I'm going to go above deck and see what's going on." He dropped his arms so she could move over and sit back down.

Her eyes narrowed slightly, but since he'd dropped his hold on her, she had to move over and sit or fall over.

He didn't give her a chance to respond to him before he climbed the narrow stairs and poked his head outside.

"Everything okay?" he asked.

"Yeah, we're heading in. The cops showed up and Joseph is dealing with the photographers," Ben told him. "How's Bella doing?"

"Good," he responded, then he glanced back just as he heard Bella throwing up. "Shit." He moved quickly and held her hair back as she lost her lunch in the small kitchen sink.

"Sorry," she sighed as she held onto the counter.

"It's okay." He felt stupid. The reason he'd kissed her to begin with was to keep her mind off the fact that she was locked below deck. "My fault."

When they docked, he rode with Adam, Lilly, Rowan, and Kayla, since they were heading his way.

He didn't get another chance to talk to Bella and was kind

of thankful for it. He needed time to cool off. Time to forget the taste and feeling of her tight body next to his.

Since their fishing trip had been cut short, he decided to try and get a few things done around his place that he'd been putting off.

There were a few boards on his back deck that needed replacing and the entire deck needed to be painted again.

By the time he was done working, the sun had sunk low in the sky. He enjoyed a cold beer on the freshly dried deck while the sun disappeared. When he made his way inside to catch the last of a game, he was surprised to see a few text messages from Ben.

Deciding he was too tired to read them, he called his friend instead.

"What's up?" he asked, putting some leftovers into the microwave.

"Did you read… never mind." Ben sighed. Ben often texted Calvin, but Calvin didn't enjoy reading the messages and almost always picked up the phone to talk instead. "Somehow, the pictures from today are already all over the web."

Calvin waited. "Shit," he added when Ben didn't say anything more.

"Cal, I'm sorry man, but it seems you made a good story," Ben added.

"What?" He frowned as he moved over to his computer. Sitting down, he pulled up the first entertainment site he found after searching Bella's name.

There on the screen was a picture of Calvin and Bella. The image had been taken seconds before he'd wrapped the towel around Bella's body. Taken out of context, the image appeared to be of a couple enjoying their time on a boat together, with him holding a towel out, waiting for Bella to step into his arms. The look on his face spoke of heat while the look on hers was clear to anyone who knew her. Fear.

"Shit," he said again.

"Yeah," Ben said.

Then Calvin read some of the headlines.

"Bella Rothschild is officially over Michael Himes. She was caught enjoying a steamy weekend on a private sailboat with her new mysterious man."

"Mysterious?" he read.

Ben chuckled. "Hey, it's better than what others are calling you."

"What?" he asked, but then he read another headline and cursed again.

"Bella's sexy and buff new man," Ben read. Then he added, "Bella Rothschild rebounds with muscular hunk."

"Hunk?" He groaned.

Ben laughed again. "It could be worse. They could have called you pudgy or soft."

"Ben." He cleared his throat trying to find the words to explain what had happened between Bella and him in the cabin.

"Don't sweat it," Ben added. "The paparazzi always get these things wrong." Calvin relaxed a little. "Hell, they claimed you and Bella were alone on the boat," Ben added.

He closed his eyes, trying to figure out what he could say to his friend. Instead, he decided to keep his mouth shut. After all, he'd talked himself into the fact that the kiss was a one-time deal.

There was no way he was going to drop his guard around Bella again. Ben had put him in charge of making sure his sister was safe, not seducing her.

"Thanks for giving me the heads-up," Calvin said.

"No problem. We figured it would be better to hear it from us than to see it on the evening news yourself."

"Shit, it's on the news?" He reached over and flipped on his set and changed the channel. Sure enough, less than a minute later, he saw the same grainy picture flash on the screen.

"Like I said, sorry." Ben chuckled. "Sit back and enjoy your five minutes of fame."

"Thanks," he said before hanging up. He had to admit, looking at the picture, he realized it was a nice shot of the pair of them. Well, if you didn't count the slight fear in Bella's eyes.

Before he could get his food from the microwave, his phone chimed again. This time, he opened the chat from Ben and smiled down at the image he'd snapped of him and Bella earlier when he'd helped her steer the boat.

The matching smiles on their faces were much better than the looks they'd given the paparazzi. He saved the image and texted back.

"Did you send this to your sister?" he asked.

"Yeah, she's the one that told us about the image spreading everywhere," Ben replied.

Shit, Calvin thought with a groan. He hadn't thought of what she must be going through. He'd seen how having her privacy invaded had affected her on the boat. He could only imagine what it would be like having her privacy constantly attacked.

Flipping his contacts open, he pulled up her number and started typing a text message.

"Sorry about all the mess today," he typed, then erased it quickly.

"Hey, I hear I'm your new sexy…" He quickly deleted it and started again.

"I'm sorry things got interrupted…" Again, he deleted his words. After all, was he talking about the kiss or the day being interrupted?

"I'm sorry your day was cut short. Don't let what happened get you down. I'll be back at work tomorrow and have ensured that no one will bother you again." He reread the message and then hit send.

Then he shot off a quick text to Stacey and Gavin. Both of them filled in for him on his days off.

"Make sure Miss Rothschild is uninterrupted. Her security is your number-one priority until I get back tomorrow morning."

Both Stacey and Gavin texted him back right away with confirmations. While he waited for a reply from Bella, he ate his leftovers and switched the set back to the end of the game.

He had just climbed out of the shower when he received a text from Bella.

"I'm sorry about all the mess I've put you in," she said.

"This is in no way on you," he responded. "Did you at least have fun today?" he asked, needing to know.

"Yes," she texted back. "Thank you for keeping my mind off… things."

He felt his loins jump at the memory of how he'd distracted her. He wanted to text back with, "Any time," but typed, "I'm sorry I didn't complete the job." He hit send before he really thought about those words. "Sorry, not what I meant," he quickly typed, feeling his entire body heat.

"LOL," she replied. "I'll take it though."

He didn't know what to say after that, so he replied, "We'll talk tomorrow when I'm back at the resort."

"See you then. Goodnight."

"Night."

The next morning, he rode the ferry to the resort with another group of employees. The daily trek was hindered only by the light rain that forced the entire group indoors.

Today it was Todd that sat behind the wheel of the large

vessel. The man was about Calvin's age and tended to flirt with all the female workers no matter what age they were.

"My mother always told me that one day I'd get in trouble," Todd had told him once. "I'd flirt with the wrong woman and end up married." He'd laughed. "Not me. I'm a perpetual bachelor."

Calvin had to admit that he'd never really believed that being a bachelor forever sounded appealing. Not that he was rushing to the altar but seeing all his friends happily married had caused him some jealous moments.

He thought it would be nice to come home to someone each night. Someone to share his life with, to raise a family with, like Ben and Sarah had.

When he stepped off the ferry, the light rain had deepened. Most of the employees raced through it to avoid getting soaked. Some shared umbrellas while others just dashed down the pathway.

Since he'd carried an umbrella that morning, he shared it with Stacey as they strolled towards the front of the resort together.

"Did you have any problems yesterday?" he asked her.

"No." She glanced at him. "We all heard about what happened on the sailboat yesterday. I can't imagine not having my privacy." She shivered.

Stacey was a middle-aged woman with three young kids at home. He couldn't remember ever seeing her not smiling or laughing. Even though she was older than him and had given birth to three kids in the past ten years, she was in better shape than he was. He knew that on her off hours she was at the gym with her husband, Eric, who was one of the police officers in Silver Cove.

When they stepped up on the front porch, he shook off his umbrella and glanced up to see Bella leaning on the railing a few feet away from them, watching him. He smiled and started to make his way towards her, when he noticed the pain in her eyes just before she turned around and moved away.

"I think she thought…" Stacey started as she touched his arm. "That we…"

He shook his head not understanding. When Stacey raised her eyebrows and motioned between them, he groaned. "Shit."

Stacey laughed. "I'm flattered, really, but you should go… explain things." She nudged him to where Bella had disappeared around the building.

"Yeah," he said and handed Stacey his umbrella.

He found Bella on the back porch and could tell she was debating rushing through the rain to make her way through the garden towards the gazebo for some privacy.

"There you are," he said, stopping beside her.

"Go away," she said, crossing her arms and turning away from the rain.

"Hey." He touched her shoulder. "What's eating you?" He knew what it was but wasn't going to try to justify his private life. After all, he'd convinced himself that whatever was between them wasn't a good idea.

He watched Bella's eyes move back to where they'd come from. "I… didn't know you were involved."

He held in his chuckle. "I'm not." His smile dropped away. He had to nip this in the bud. He couldn't keep leading her on. Bella was his best friends' little sister. At that thought, he swayed slightly away from her.

"You aren't?" she asked, her eyes going to his.

The look in her eyes caused his heart to jump in his chest. She was wearing a large gray sweater over a white tank top with gray leggings that hugged her every curve. Her long hair was flowing around her face and shoulders. He wanted to reach up and bury his fingers in the dark tresses as he pulled those plump lips to his.

He shook the thoughts of kissing her from his mind.

"No," he answered and forced his eyes from her. "Have you had breakfast yet?" he asked, realizing suddenly that they were standing within view of the large windows in the dining room. He could see guests enjoying their breakfast inside already.

Her gaze followed his. "No, I was hoping we could talk."

He glanced at his watch. "I have a staff meeting first, but I can meet you inside after."

She nodded slightly as she glanced down at her hands. "I... I'm not the jealous type."

He sighed. "Bella, we..." Just then his cell phone chimed with his reminder about the staff meeting. "Later." He touched her shoulder.

When she nodded, he followed her inside and, as she was seated, he disappeared down the stairs towards his meeting.

CHAPTER NINE

od how stupid could she be? When she'd watched Calvin and the pretty brunette that worked the front desk making their way slowly through the rain, huddled together under the umbrella, she'd been instantly hurt.

She'd been cheated on before and didn't like the feeling. Not that she and Calvin were officially… what? Seeing each other? Dating?

She rolled her eyes and lifted the menu slightly to hide the motion from everyone else in the room.

"Ready?" A pretty blonde waitress stopped by her table.

"Yes, I'll have the French Toast Fosters." She set the menu down. She'd been dreaming of the sweet breakfast and figured she might as well enjoy herself since she didn't know how much longer she would be at the resort.

"Great choice," the woman said, taking up her menu. But then she leaned closer. "I just wanted to say that I'm such a huge fan of yours." Her smile widened. "'Running Home' is one of my favorite songs." She sighed. "It's the reason I came back to Silver Cove." She shook her head. "Anyway, if you need anything else… just let me know. I'm Chrissy."

"Thank you, Chrissy." Bella smiled and watched the woman disappear.

Those were the kind of fan interactions Bella enjoyed the most. She didn't mind the occasional fan rushing to her for an autograph or a selfie. After all, she loved her fan base. They were the reason she was where she was today. She owed them everything.

It was the paparazzi she could do without. The tabloid articles filled with conspiracies about her that had zero truth to them drove her crazy.

She ate her breakfast, pouring over the news and her social media feeds as she enjoyed the food. Rumors were running wild as fans scrambled to ask her who her mysterious hunk was.

Some even wished her well on her vacation. There were hundreds of well-wishers. Then there were the others. Fans outraged that she would break things off with Michael. Some even telling her that they were meant to be and that she shouldn't have cheated on Michael.

A handful called her names. She blocked them or reported them when they crossed the line. It was strange, she'd always been for the freedom of expressing yourself. But when it came to her private life and her feelings, when someone called her a slut or a bitch because she wouldn't date the man they wanted, she wished everyone could understand how much it hurt.

After blocking about half a dozen of them, she gave up and set her phone down to look around the dining room.

The large party from the other day had left, leaving the place feeling almost empty. She wondered when the next big party would be arriving and glanced out the windows just as a bolt of lightning brightened the sky.

She'd missed the weather around here. The snow in the winters, the rain and cooler weather in the spring and summers. Not that she hadn't enjoyed the warmth of California, but every now and then she wanted a rainy day to keep her indoors.

"It's supposed to get worse later today," Calvin said, breaking into her thoughts.

She glanced over and smiled. "It's a good thing yesterday was sunny. I'd hate to be out on the water in this."

He motioned, asking if he could sit. She nodded and moved her empty plates towards the edge of the table. Chrissy rushed over and removed them.

"More coffee?" she asked.

"Sure," Bella answered.

"Boss man?" Chrissy asked with a smile and a sparkle in her eyes.

"Thanks." He nodded.

"She has a crush on you," Bella said, leaning forward.

"She does?" Calvin frowned and watched the pretty blonde disappear to get their drinks. "How can you tell?"

She chuckled. "A woman knows." She sighed and leaned back.

"She's just a kid." He was still frowning.

"Oh yeah, sure, what is she? Twenty? Twenty-one?" Bella laughed.

"I mean…" Calvin sighed and then shook his head. "Never mind. How are you holding up?" he asked her.

Her eyebrows shot up. "Holding up?"

"With all the…" He waved his hands towards her phone, as if the motion would explain everything.

"It's not the first time I've had the paparazzi snap pictures and make assumptions about my love life," she said easily. "The real question is"—she leaned forward again— "how are you holding up?"

Just then, Chrissy came back and set their coffee down. "Let me know if you need anything else." She disappeared again.

"Has fame gone to your head already?" she joked. "I mean, being labeled—what was it? Oh, yes—a mysterious hunk, has its perks."

He rolled his eyes. "I've never really thought of myself as the hunk type."

She smiled. "No?" She ran her eyes over him slowly, immediately disagreeing with his assessment of himself. He was very much a hunk. She remembered how his arms and chest had felt against her own. Seeing all those tan muscles that he hid under the dress clothes he wore now. "As a member of the opposite sex, I can officially say that you fit the hunk bill."

He chuckled slightly. "Okay, so I'm assuming the news of our little outing yesterday will pass over quickly?"

Her smile slipped a little. "Until there's new gossip to go around, I'm afraid everyone will be trying to figure out who you are. My agent thinks it might be best to come right out and give the press your information and make a statement." It was why she'd been waiting for him on the front porch earlier. Maggie was putting together a statement right now for him to approve. Just in case.

When Calvin remained silent, she bit her bottom lip and waited as he thought it through.

"What do you think?" he asked, his eyes running over her face.

She shrugged and finished her coffee. "It does stand to reason that if you give them something, they wouldn't dig as deeply." She watched his eyes darken as he tensed.

"Then go ahead." He moved to stand up. "Either way, at least it will clear things up that we're nothing but friends." He took his mug and she surprised him by standing up with him.

"Are we?" she asked, their bodies brushing.

His eyes darkened slightly just before he stepped away. "That's all we can be." He nodded to her. "Now, if you'll excuse me. I have work."

She watched him disappear through a doorway and mentally kicked herself. Well, that could have gone better, she thought to herself as she looked around the room.

She didn't want to head back up to her room to be alone anymore. Yesterday evening she'd spent enough time alone after she'd returned to the resort after the sailboat incident. Deciding she could use a walk, she headed upstairs to grab a jacket and change into her rain boots.

Even though the rain hadn't let up when she stepped out onto the porch, she tucked her hair under her hood and made her way across the yard. Since she was the only one crazy enough to venture out into the storm, she had the gardens all to herself. She didn't mind the rain. You just had to have the mindset that, no matter what you did, you were going to get wet and that you were one hot shower away from recovering from the droplets.

Actually, the foul weather gave her plenty of time to think as she strolled through the gardens. The fog had yet to lift from the grounds, leaving her shadowed in mist.

Hugging her jacket closer to her, she found the bench along the rocky shoreline empty and sat to enjoy the stormy view of the water crashing below her.

She sat out there until she felt a shiver race up her spine, then she slowly started making her way back inside. She had just stepped into the garden when another shiver raced through her, one that had nothing to do with the chill in the air. She'd felt this one so many times before that she knew instantly that she was being watched. Thinking it was another guest out for a walk, she glanced around.

Since spring had filled all the bushes with flowers and thick branches covered in green leaves, it was almost impossible to see through them to notice if someone was around. The pathways were the only clear way to see around her.

"Hello?" she called out. Instantly, she heard a low chuckle and tensed. "Who's there?" she demanded, taking a step back. Another low chuckle sounded from somewhere in the fog. This one sounded a little closer than the last and was coming from another direction. It was as if she was surrounded.

"You thought you could hide from me, bitch?" The voice was so low, she had to strain to hear the words.

Before the last of the sentence was out, she was racing down the slick pathway. She skidded once on the wet pavement and landed on her hands and knees but didn't stop to register the pain of her torn skin before she jumped up and rushed towards the back patio.

Taking the back stairs two at a time, she yanked open the door only to bump into a solid chest. She cried out and started fighting the arms that wrapped around her until she heard Calvin's voice.

"What's wrong?" he asked her, holding her still.

"Someone…" She looked up at him and he must have seen the fear in her eyes, because his arms tightened around her. "Someone was in the garden."

Calvin's eyebrows shot up. "Did they hurt you?"

"No, they… someone was there," she repeated.

He frowned and looked at her face. "It is a public garden." He shook his head.

"They…" She closed her eyes and took a deep breath. "They said… things. And laughed at me and hid in the mist."

Calvin glanced towards the doors and then around the lobby. "Gavin." He motioned towards a man that Bella had seen behind the front desk a few times. "Take a stroll around the garden. Let me know who is out there."

"Sure thing, boss." Gavin grabbed a large umbrella and walked by them. "You might want to clean those cuts," Gavin pointed out as he passed them.

Calvin's eyes moved over her, and he gasped when he noticed her torn leggings and bleeding hands.

"You're hurt." His fingers tightened on her arms. Then he was lifting her in his arms and carrying her down the hallway.

At some point during her race out of the garden, her hood must have fallen, leaving her soaking-wet hair clinging to her face. She must look a mess.

The stinging in her knees and hands finally registered through the chill of her skin the moment he set her down on the edge of a large desk. She hadn't even had time to enjoy the feeling of being in his arms since he'd rushed her up the stairs and down the hallway so quickly.

She'd been in this office plenty of times before. It was a larger office shared by her brother and Sarah.

After depositing her on the desktop, Calvin rushed around and opened the closet and came back with a white box and set it beside her.

"Here, let me take a look at these." He pulled her hands gently into his own. He helped her remove her wet jacket and tossed it over the back of the chair. His dark head bent over her hands as he cleaned the grit from her skin.

She winced a few times and hissed at the pain, but each time he would still and gently blow on her skin, soothing the pain away.

"How did this happen?" he asked once the worst of the dirt was cleared away.

"I slipped on the wet pathway," she admitted, feeling stupid. She was even questioning if she'd just imagined the voice or if someone had really been there. After all, it had been so light, she'd had to strain to hear the words on the breeze.

"Did you see who it was?" he asked her, his eyes on the cuts on her palms.

"No." She closed her eyes and held in a groan.

"Hey." He gently touched her thigh just above the tears in the light material. Her eyes opened and met his. She could see worry and fear behind them and relaxed slightly. "We'll figure this out." He gave her a slight smile.

"I'm not crazy." She didn't know why she said it, but just hearing her shaky voice say those words had her rolling her eyes. "Okay, that totally sounded nuts, but I didn't imagine it. Someone laughed at me and said—"

Just then, there was a knock on the office door.

"Come in," Calvin called out.

Gavin opened the door and stepped in. "The garden's all clear. I couldn't find anyone." He held out a phone. "I found this on the path though." He handed the phone to Calvin.

"My phone." She reached for it. "I must have dropped it when I fell."

Calvin handed it to her. "Thanks," he said to Gavin, dismissing the man. Once they were alone in the office again, Calvin turned back towards her. "Let me take a look at your knees."

He gently touched the ruined gray leggings and tried to peek through the slits to her marred skin. When it was apparent he wouldn't be able to clean through the material, she nudged him aside and stood quickly, pulling off her boots and removing the leggings. She hissed when the material stuck to the blood dripping from the cuts. Sitting back down on the desk, she motioned to her knees.

"There, now you can work unhindered." She was wearing a pair of pink-and-black striped boy short underwear underneath the thick gray leggings. Calvin had seen her in a skimpier outfit yesterday. Besides, she was squeamish when it came to cleaning up her wounds. There was no way she would be able to get all the dirt and pebbles out herself.

His eyes moved over her slowly, but when she held still, he started working on the cuts on her knees.

"Are you doing okay?" he asked when she winced for the tenth time.

"Yes, just don't stop." She closed her eyes and gripped the edge of the desk. Here, the pain was twice what it had been on her hands. Obviously, her knees had taken most of her weight when she'd fallen.

As he worked this time, she leaned back and tried to think of anything except the pain.

"Why would you think I wouldn't believe you?" he asked as his hands worked. Her eyes opened and she looked down at him. He was watching her, his hands hovering over her skin, holding a bandage.

"No reason," she started to say, but his eyebrows shot up, and she could tell he knew she was about to lie. Instead, she shrugged. "When I thought someone had followed me home one night, everyone thought I had just imagined it." She sighed.

"No one believed you?" he asked, gently putting the bandage over the cuts on her right knee.

"No." She shook her head. "They all said that I had just spooked myself." She relaxed as he opened another bandage for her other knee. "I convinced myself that I had imagined it all."

"Did you?"

She thought about it for a moment and then shook her head.

"No, I don't think I did." She shrugged.

"There," he said, finishing putting the bandage on her

knee. "It's stopped bleeding." He stood up and helped her down from the desk.

Just then, the office door flew open, and Bella winced when her brother stepped inside. The look on Ben's face told her everything. Her brother was pissed. And when his eyes moved towards Calvin, she knew why Calvin was having such a tough time being with her.

"What's this all about…" Ben's words dropped away when he noticed her holding Calvin's hand in just her underwear. "What the what?" Her brother's eyes heated and before she could stop him, he punched Calvin right in the jaw.

CHAPTER TEN

*S*hit. He supposed he deserved the blow. He braced for another punch, willing to take it, since his mind hadn't been all too pure moments before Ben had interrupted them.

"Ben!" Bella cried out. She shoved her body between the two men. She was still only dressed in a white tank top and those sexy boy shorts while he stood fully dressed for work. "He was helping me," she said, shoving her hands into her brother's chest. "I fell and he was bandaging me up."

She held up her hands to her brother and then motioned to her knees, where he'd placed the bandages over her red and bloody skin moments before.

Ben jerked his eyes away from Calvin's face. After seeing the bandages, he relaxed. "Shit." He pushed his hands through his hair and looked back to Calvin. "Someone had said..." He sighed and closed his eyes.

Knowing his best friend had, for even a moment, believed that Calvin could hurt Bella, or anyone for that matter, stung worse than his bruised jaw. Still, he knew Ben wasn't thinking straight. He'd probably heard that his sister had been injured.

"Sorry, man." Ben closed his eyes. "Dude, she's my sister."

Calvin felt his heart fall and nodded. "I know." He couldn't stop the guilty look nor could he deny the attraction he felt for Bella.

"If you two… chauvinist pigs are done…" Bella said, storming over to yank her leggings on quickly. He reached out his hand to steady her when she almost fell over, but Ben rushed to her side to help her. Calvin stepped back and averted his eyes from the sexy pink underwear. Bella slapped her brother's hands away and, after covering herself again, bent over to pick up her boots and jacket. "Now, if the two of you are done trying to control my life, I'm heading upstairs for a hot bath." Her eyes landed on Calvin, and he shrunk back as her eyes narrowed at him. Then she turned to Ben. "I am my own woman. What I do and with whom I do it is none of your business." She stormed out of the office, slamming the door behind her.

"We fucked that up." Ben sighed as he ran his hands through his hair again.

"We?" Calvin asked.

Ben turned on him, and he could see all the anger and worry was gone. "I'm sorry," he added quickly. "I shouldn't have jumped to conclusions. I'd heard that she'd been hurt and well… she's my sister. You know how that feels."

The words stung more than the punch had, so he nodded. "I kissed Bella yesterday," he blurted out. "So, I deserved it."

Ben's eyes narrowed, then he closed them and took a couple of deep breaths.

"She's right. It's none of my business. So, whatever," he said when he opened them again.

Calvin balked. "That's it?"

"What do you want? I've already punched you." He motioned to Calvin's bruised jaw.

Calvin reached up and wiggled it for good measure. "Yeah, but you hit like a—"

"Careful," Ben warned with a chuckle. "We both know who punches better between us."

Calvin shut his mouth. "Fine, but like I said, I deserved it and more. You're right, she was alone with me in nothing but…"

"Don't mention it." Ben moved closer to him and he flinched for show. "Ever again. Tell you what, just promise you won't hurt her." He leaned closer and lowered his voice. "Because if you do, there'll be a lot more than a hurt jaw to show for it."

"What are you saying?" Calvin asked.

"I'm not saying anything." Ben moved towards the door. "Except…" He glanced back at him. "Watch out for her and don't piss me off." He turned and left.

Calvin sat on the edge of the desk and replayed the last hour in his mind. Remembering Bella's words had him thinking he was in bigger trouble than he'd first believed.

He decided to check out the garden himself and stepped outside to the heavy rain. He took his time going over every inch of the grounds. From what Gavin had told him about where he'd found Bella's phone, he gauged that someone could have hidden behind a large hydrangea tree without being seen. To be honest, there were so many hiding places in the gardens that a dozen people could be hiding from him at that very moment.

He went back inside and spent the next hour scouring the guest list. He ran the standard security checks that he used for new hires on some of them.

He didn't think there could be a paparazzo in the bunch,

but then again, he didn't think people registered to stalk the famous. By the time the dinner hour rolled around, he figured he needed to head up and apologize to Bella. He'd heard from Stacey that Bella had ordered room service for lunch. He didn't expect her downstairs for dinner either, but he looked for her the entire meal.

Before he was due to head out on the ferry, he climbed the stairs, thinking of exactly what he was going to say to her. He stood outside of her door for a few minutes, coming up with the right words, and was just about to knock on her door when it flew open.

She stood there in a pair of black leggings and a light gray sweater that almost went down to her knees. The sweater hung off one shoulder, exposing the soft skin to his view.

"I wondered how long you were going to stand out there," she said, leaning against the door.

He dropped his hand and cleared his throat. "I, um, wanted to apologize." He tucked his hands in his pockets. When she didn't respond, he shifted his feet. "For earlier."

"I can choose whom I'm with and whom I'm not." She narrowed her eyes.

He swallowed and nodded. "Yes, ma'am, you can."

She smiled quickly, grabbed his tie, and pulled him into the room. He was so dumbfounded that he didn't fight her. Hell, what she was doing didn't even register until her lips were covering his as she pushed him up against the door to her room.

Then his brain shut off completely as her mouth slanted over his and her soft body pushed against his. His hands moved up to her shoulders, holding her. He wasn't sure if he was pulling her closer to him or pushing her away, since he could no longer tell up from down.

She mixed everything up in his mind. All his carefully laid

plans flew out the window when she kissed him. When he tasted her, he completely lost control.

"Bella," he said between breaths.

"No, don't think," she said as she leaned back, her eyes meeting his. "Tell me you don't want this as much as I do," she said with a slight warning.

He couldn't lie to her, but he doubted he could find his voice and just shook his head.

"No?" she asked, tilting her head. "No, you don't want this." She waved her hand between them.

He took a deep breath to clear his mind, but he got a whiff of her sexy perfume and groaned. Instead of answering, he reached for her and pulled her close. This time it was his turn to take control. Her body pressed up against his, and he reversed their positions until he had her up against the door. Her hands moved slowly over his shoulders.

His mouth moved over hers and then moved down her neck. He pushed her hair to the side, giving him better access so he could trail kisses down to her exposed shoulder. He nudged the sweater down even further and then pulled the long hem of the sweater up and over her head. She was completely bare underneath, and he almost came instantly seeing how perfect she was. Dipping his head, he trailed his tongue over her, enjoying how her nipples peaked for him.

Her fingers dug into his hair as she held him to her skin.

"Cal," she sighed and arched even more against the closed door. "Please." She reached for his shirt and winced when she bunched it in her injured hands.

"Here." He pulled away and took her hands in his, looking at the bandages he'd placed earlier. Lifting her palms up to his lips, he placed kisses on each one before stepping back and pulling off his shirt for her.

Her eyes ran over him, and he could see the heat as she

sucked her bottom lip between her teeth. When she reached out and brushed the back of her hand down his chest, it was his turn to arch into her touch.

"Bella." He meant it as a warning.

She looked up into his eyes and reached for his hands, then she walked him towards her bedroom. He'd been in the room many times. He'd been in almost every room at the resort for inspections.

The large bed appeared as if she'd napped in it. Its blankets were pushed back and there was a laptop sitting on the small desk across the room. He noticed she was a tidy guest.

She stopped at the foot of the bed and turned back to him. His eyes moved back to her perfect breasts, and she chuckled.

"God." He closed his eyes. "I can't think when I'm around you."

"Good, now you know how I feel." She wrapped her arms around him and pushed her naked skin up against his.

He sighed at the feeling of her soft skin against his. He could feel her nipples poking him as he ran his hands over her soft curves.

"Touch me," she said. She laid her lips on his collarbone.

He couldn't have denied her at this point. She'd brought him far beyond his breaking point.

"Tell me you have protection," he groaned as her mouth ran over him.

"Nightstand." She flicked her tongue over his flat nipple.

"Thank god." He buried his fingers into her hair. When she ran her mouth over his stomach, he sucked in his breath. "Bella," he warned, trying to nudge her away.

"Shush, I'm hungry." She smiled up at him.

"Vixen." He chuckled as she reached for his belt. She tossed it across the room, and he laughed. Then she bit her bottom lip while she unzipped his slacks.

"You're going to kill me," he warned.

"Good." She slid his pants down. "My god," she sighed as his erection sprang free. His eyes closed as she ran her fingers softly over him. He couldn't help jumping slightly when she laid a soft kiss over him.

When she ran her tongue from the base of his shaft to the tip, he growled and gripped her under her arms before flipping her onto the bed. She laughed and reached for him, but he pulled back. He grabbed her leggings and slowly slid them down her legs as he bent over and trailed his mouth over the smoothness of her legs.

When she was free of all clothing, he yanked open the nightstand drawer and pulled out a condom. "There is a god," he said as he came back to her. Instead of sheathing himself and embedding himself in her slickness, he bent between her legs and ran his mouth over her. She cried out his name when he flicked his tongue over her pussy.

Her hands buried in his hair as he lapped at her, enjoying the sweetness of her.

"You taste so good," he groaned as she wrapped her legs around his shoulders. "Come for me," he said softly. "I can't wait to taste you on my tongue." He slid his tongue into her slickness as she arched her back and gripped the comforter. The soft sexy sounds she was making only had him growing harder for her.

"Yes," he encouraged. "Let go," he said as he slowly slid a finger into her. When he felt her tense and cry out, he smiled at the richness of her and enjoyed it for a moment before pulling back and sliding on the condom.

"Look at me," he said as he settled between her spread legs.

"Calvin." She wrapped her arms around him. "Please."

He smiled. "Hold onto me," he begged as he slid slowly

into her. She was tight and warm and everything he'd ever dreamed she'd be.

When they started moving together, he bent down and kissed her until he exploded for her as she cried out his name again.

CHAPTER ELEVEN

She was floating on a cloud. God. Had she ever had sex as good as this before? No. Not even close.

She smiled up into the darkness and stretched her arms over her head.

"Now you've done it," Calvin said from beside her in the darkness of the room.

"Hm?" She turned slightly to see his outline.

"How am I going to explain why I missed the ferry?" He rolled over and his hand came up to rest on her waist, slowly moving over her hip, causing her to want him again.

"Surely you work late all the time?" She moved closer to him and ran her hand over his chest, wincing slightly as her palms stung. She wished she didn't have the stupid bandages so she could feel him under her skin.

"I do, but since there aren't any big groups here currently, it's going to be obvious why I stayed behind. Especially since word got out about Ben finding us… earlier."

"Word got out?" She frowned and stilled.

"Yeah," he sighed. "Linda happened to be passing by the office when everything went down. She overheard it all and, well, everyone who works at the resort knows what happened." He glanced around and shrugged. "I wouldn't be surprised if someone saw me coming up here earlier."

"So." She shrugged. "Who cares?" She relaxed slightly. "I mean the entire world believes that we're lovers already."

"True." He chuckled as one of his hands moved up to cup her while the other moved lower. "So, what you're saying is… we shouldn't fight this." He touched her and her eyes slid closed as he slid a finger into her again.

"No." She enjoyed the feeling of him pinching her nipple as he entered her with a finger over and over.

"Do you like that?" he teased.

"Yes." She moved slightly when he nudged her legs wider.

"How much do you like it?" he asked. "If I was to…" He pulled his hands away and she made a soft noise. He chuckled and returned his hand to between her thighs. Then his mouth covered her breasts, and he sucked her nipple and rolled his tongue around it.

"This," he said, "right here. You taste like cotton candy." She chuckled and pushed her fingers into his hair. His mouth moved over her as she heard him open another condom wrapper. She'd been lucky she still had a box of them in her overnight case.

Just before he slid it on, she moved swiftly until he lay beneath her. "My turn." She smiled down at him, taking the condom from him.

He held still as she ran her mouth over him, down his chest, stopping to enjoy his flat nipples and all those sexy muscles, which were covered with a light dusting of dark hair. When she took him into her mouth, he tensed while his fingers dug into her hair.

"My god, Bella." He groaned as she moved up and down his length, enjoying how hard he was, how perfect he felt.

When he nudged her up, she sat up and slowly slid the condom over him before climbing to sit across his thighs.

His eyes raked over her, then he reached up and touched her breasts as he pulled her down onto his full length.

"Perfect," he sighed as she embedded him fully in her heat. It was even more perfect than before.

She had expected him to fall asleep after such a perfect moment, but just as she was drifting off to sleep, he rolled out of the bed.

"Don't tell me you're going to leave?" she asked.

"Yup," he sighed as he slid on his shoes.

She must have fallen asleep. He'd turned on the hall light so as to not wake her. She'd only woken when she'd reached for him and found his side of the bed cold.

"It wouldn't do if I showed up to work in the morning in the same clothes I wore today." He chuckled. "Besides, I've already texted JT." He glanced at his phone. "He's going to pick me up in five minutes." He stood up, leaned over the bed, and kissed her. "Go back to sleep."

"Calvin," she said as he turned away.

"Hm?" he asked from the doorway.

"I don't regret being with you," she said with a smile.

He nodded. "Me either. Night," he said as he left.

She snuggled back into the bed, pulling the pillow he'd used close to her face to enjoy the lingering scent of him as she fell back to sleep.

She woke to her phone chiming and was going to ignore it, but then it exploded with notifications.

Groaning, she rolled over and grabbed it, yanking the cable from the charger as she peered at the screen, blinking a few times until her eyes adjusted.

She sat up quickly and gasped. With shaky fingers, she swiped through the images.

When her phone rang in her hands, she jumped and

squealed, then answered it when she saw Maggie's face appear on the screen.

"Tell me this can be controlled," she said before Maggie could say anything.

"I was hoping you'd have some insight as to what we could do to stop this," Maggie replied with a sigh.

Bella glanced at the clock and estimated that it was just past five in the morning for Maggie.

Sitting up, she pulled her iPad to her lap and flipped it open. "Is it everywhere?" she asked.

"I'm afraid so. The sun isn't even up here. All the notifications woke me." She heard her agent yawn.

"Well, there's nothing we can do right now. Get some more rest. I'll think it over and see what I can come up with." Bella closed her eyes and wished she could go back and kick Michael in the balls the last time she'd seen him.

"Okay, if you need anything…" Maggie added.

"Outside of a hitman?" she joked, causing Maggie to chuckle. "Call me when you're fully awake."

"Will do," Maggie said before hanging up.

Bella scoured the full interview Michael had given an online magazine, which had gone live first thing that morning.

She didn't know what upset her more, the fact that he disclosed some of the stuff she'd said to him or the fact that he accused her of harassing him and stalking him.

When her phone rang an hour later, she had almost worked herself into a panic as all the hate comments started flooding in on her social media.

Her brother's voice did little to soothe her as he tried to convince her that it would blow over and that she should do her interview.

Maggie had suggested the same thing, but she didn't think that fighting fire with fire was the road she wanted to take.

Besides, Michael was an established Hollywood staple. She was only an up-and-coming singing star with one successful album under her belt. Why would anyone believe her story over his?

The things he'd said in the interview made it seem like she was a nutjob. When asked about the picture of her and Calvin on the boat, Michael had laughed it off as a stunt to throw the media off her crazy trail. He produced some of her text messages to him, which were taken completely out of context. He even tried to convince everyone that the texts were from that same day she'd been on the boat with Calvin.

The fact was, she'd only texted him a handful of times, since they'd only gone to three events together. After that, he'd been the one to text her and her responses were usually one sentence long.

"We're going to come there for lunch," Ben told her. "We'll help you figure something out."

"No," she told him, "don't. You guys were planning on going to Boston this week. Don't change your plans for me. Besides, I've found the perfect hiding place, and Calvin is here to watch out for me." She smiled remembering last night.

"Fine." Her brother sighed loudly. "What do you want me to tell the folks?"

Bella groaned. "We both know whatever you say to them won't matter."

"Yeah." Ben sighed. "Okay, if you need us, we're only a call and a short helicopter flight away. I'm going to call Calvin now and make sure he has your back while we're gone."

She smiled. Oh, Calvin had her back all right. She held in a chuckle. "Thanks," she added. "Have a safe trip. I'm sure the folks will be so busy loving the girls that they won't even ask about me."

"Isn't it funny? As parents go, they sucked royally, but as grandparents… They dote on the girls."

"It's a good thing," she admitted. "Your girls enjoy them. That's all that matters."

"Okay, see you in a week," Ben added before hanging up.

She slid out of bed and walked into the bathroom to get ready to head down for brunch. She was starving and didn't want to eat alone in her room again.

Taking her time to prepare herself to see Calvin again, she dressed in a striped blue cotton romper and tied her long hair to one side with a loose French braid. She checked to make sure her makeup was perfectly in place then grabbed her iPad and headed downstairs.

It was so hard not to immediately look around for Calvin when she stepped into the dining room. She was seated in the booth along the windows and had just placed her order when Calvin strolled in talking to a young couple holding a small child.

He looked so relaxed and comfortable talking to the couple. That was, until he spotted her. Then she saw heat flood his eyes. Moments later, he excused himself and made his way across the room towards her.

"Good morning." He smiled down at her.

She motioned for him to take the seat across from her. "Morning." She smiled back at him.

"Sleep well?" he asked.

"I did. You?" She sipped her coffee, hoping that it would soothe her throat.

He nodded, then his smile slipped a little. "Your brother called."

"Yeah." She nodded. "It's a mess."

"I agree with Ben. Maybe you should go on the record." He waved the waiter away when he approached them. "Nothing for me today, Eddie."

The man frowned, then nodded and quickly disappeared.

"I'm not sure." She sighed and glanced out the window. "Then it's a her-word-against-his sort of deal. If I remain silent, I'm hoping this will all just… blow over."

He shrugged and looked down at her hands. "I guess it was a lot easier on you being romantically linked to me than him."

She laughed. "Yes, it was."

He smiled and reached his hand across the table and took hers. "We could always give them another story." Just then his phone rang, and he sighed. "Which we will have to work on later. We've got another party coming in for this weekend."

She squeezed his hand. "Later then."

She couldn't explain it, but after her talk with Cal, she felt more settled. Like she could conquer anything. Even an egotistical, stalking director with the entire world on his side.

She'd just finished up her brunch when Maggie called her back.

So?" Maggie asked. "Did you read it yet?"

"Read what?"

"Check your email."

Bella flipped open her iPad and looked at the proposed statement Maggie had emailed her.

"It's tasteful and doesn't go into too much detail. I'm not sure it will keep the reporters at bay, but at least it won't have them knocking down my door with torches. I guess we can go ahead with it."

Maggie sighed loudly. "I'm sorry I ever connected the two of you. That is the last time I interfere with my client's private lives."

"Hey," Bella broke in, "you had no clue. After all, there aren't any warning labels for men."

Maggie laughed. "If there were, the last three men I've gone out on dates with would've had plenty of them."

Bella smiled. "Go ahead and send it out. I'll post it on all my social media pages."

"I can arrange for an interview there at the resort if you want. All you have to do is say the word," Maggie added.

"No, thank you. For now, let's see how the statement plays out."

CHAPTER TWELVE

Calvin spent his entire workday wishing he could hunt Bella down and talk to her. There was so much he wanted to assure her of after Ben's call.

The first thing he'd done was lock himself in his office and read Michael Himes entire interview. He'd believed he hated the man before, but after reading the narcissistic interview he wanted to smash the man's teeth in.

The man had accused Bella of setting up the meeting so she could get an audience with him. Then he said that, shortly after he'd called off their relationship, she'd turned to stalking him, going as far as following him and sending crazy text messages to him.

He'd promised Ben that he'd watch over Bella. He had almost come clean about the night before but figured that Ben had meant it when he'd told him he didn't want to know what was going on between them.

Knowing that most of the group for the large wedding party was arriving, he made his way down to the dock to collect the guests in the six-seater golf cart they had on the island. It helped with some of the older guests or the ones with kids.

The luggage would be delivered up to the main building by a few employees driving the used luggage truck Sarah had purchased a year ago from the airport. The thing had earned its position as one of the best buys so far. He remembered when they had to take several trips up to the building from the dock, trying to fit all the luggage on the golf cart.

When the ferry arrived, more than twenty people stepped off it, demanding his attention.

"Welcome to East Haven," he said with a warm smile. He got everyone's attention. "No, please," he said to a woman trying to cart her luggage off the ferry. "Please, leave all your luggage. We'll take care of getting your bags up to your rooms." The woman set her bag down. "If you haven't already attached a luggage tag with your name, please take a moment to do so now so we can make sure your bags get to the correct rooms." He waved towards the small luggage cards that East Haven Resorts had printed out. Several people moved forward to take them.

"Once you're done, feel free to head on up to the main building. If anyone in your party needs help, you will be shuttled up." He motioned to the golf cart.

An attractive middle-aged blonde woman approached him. "I'm Kathleen Wright. Mother of the bride." She smiled at him. "My daughter, Eliza." She motioned to a pretty young blonde woman, who smiled shyly at him. "I assume every-thing is ready for us?"

"Yes, Mrs. Wright," he responded.

"Miss," the woman corrected as she ran her eyes over him.

"Miss." He nodded quickly. "Yes, everything is all set." He motioned towards the cart. "If you want, I can take you up to the main building?"

The woman smiled. "No, I think we're going to walk

around and see the grounds before we head in. It was a long flight and drive here."

He stepped aside and waved to a pathway. "The path towards the gazebo is there."

For the next hour, he answered questions, shuttled guests, and made sure everyone was checked in and had gotten to the right rooms. He met the groom, a Fredrick Stafford. The man was easily twice the age of the young bride and somewhat of a jerk.

Calvin caught the guy yelling at one of the maids in the hallway just outside his rooms.

"Can I help you?" Calvin had stepped in.

The man's eyes had run up and down him quickly.

"I would hope so." The silver-haired man had crossed his arms over his rather large belly. "There are only four towels in my room. I specifically demanded that six be placed in here before I arrived."

Sandra, the maid who Fredrick had been yelling at, turned to him. "I was just bringing these up." She held out two more towels."

"Thank you." He took the towels from Sandra himself and turned to the man.

"I'm sure, Mr...."

"Fredrick Stafford, the groom," he answered, puffing out his chest.

That statement took Calvin by surprise and it was obvious to the man, even though Calvin liked to think he recovered quickly enough. "Mr. Stafford, it was just a slight oversight. If you'd just let me know…"

"Slight?" The man's voice had risen. "If you believe that this is slight, I wonder how the rest of the wedding is going to go? I knew it was a mistake to trust the Wrights with something so important as finding the venue for my special day."

His special day? Calvin thought, but he held his tongue as the man continued to belittle the resort and staff.

After leaving the man, he made his way towards his office, intent on taking a couple of aspirin for the headache he had gained from listening to the man complaining.

He hadn't expected to see Kathleen Wright standing just outside his office.

"May I help you?" he asked as he approached her.

She turned and smiled warmly at him. "Yes, Mr. Winters, I was told this was your office." She shifted towards him slightly. "I was hoping you and I could have a little chat about the plans."

Another hour later, he wondered if the woman was just trying to fill her boring evening. At first, she'd gone over a written list. But after marking off each item on the list, she'd started chatting about her daughter and how hard it had been raising the girl on her own.

He was thankful when his office phone rang, giving him an excuse to end the impromptu meeting, even if it was a call because the maintenance shed had been broken into and several tools were missing. Dealing with missing items was far better than dealing with the bride's mother who was obviously trying to flirt with him.

When he met Kevin at the shed in question, he knew it was far more than just a few tools that had gone missing. The entire shed had been gone through. It appeared someone had been tossing tools around as if looking for what they needed.

"What's missing?" he asked the man.

"A pair of bolt clippers, a ladder, and some shears." Kevin shook his head. "It doesn't make sense. They left the expensive tools." He motioned towards the chainsaw and other power tools.

"Probably some kids." He glanced around. "They couldn't

have gone far. Let's check the grounds." He pulled out his walkie talkie and called for backup.

For the next two hours, he and every other free employee scoured the grounds. They found the ladder leaning against the side of the employees' building, as if someone had snuck up to the second floor. He made a mental note of which window it was sitting outside of before dragging the heavy thing back to the shed.

He heard they'd found the bolt clippers outside of the pool house. But since nothing had been disturbed there, he figured whoever had taken them hadn't realized they had installed electric key locks a few years back.

In order to get in and out of the other buildings, they had to have an employee key pass.

"We haven't found the shears yet," Kevin told him. "We'll keep an eye out for them." He glanced down at his watch. "It's almost the end of the shift."

Calvin glanced down at his watch and realized he'd missed lunch. Hell, the entire day had gone by without his notice. Well, except for the hour where the bride's mother had droned on.

He glanced back up at the main building and looked to where Bella's rooms were. He could see her standing out on the balcony, talking on her phone. It appeared she was arguing with someone, since she was pacing back and forth waving her arms.

"Got it bad for that one." Kevin slapped him on the back. "Is it weird that the whole world knows?"

Calvin groaned. "We're not…" He realized what he'd been about to say, but then remembered last night and shut his mouth. Kevin laughed and slapped him again on the shoulder.

"Whatever, bro. We can all see the way you two look at

each other. I used to look at my wife like that, right up until she cheated on me with my best friend."

"Ouch." Calvin turned to him and shook his head.

"I'm better off. Now he gets to listen to her nag about everything." Kevin shook his head as he moved away. "We'll keep an eye out for the shears. I'm sure they'll show up. You may want to keep your eyes out for guests who could be bored enough to do something like this."

"Right." Calvin nodded and started walking towards the building.

His movement caused Bella to glance down and, when she noticed him, she smiled for a split second. Then whoever was on the phone with her said something, and she frowned and went inside.

He headed back to his office and groaned silently when he saw that the young bride was standing outside his door, waiting for him. She was nervously wringing her hands.

"Miss Wright, how can I help you?" he asked as he opened his door for her.

"Mr. Winters, I was hoping you had a moment…" She glanced over her shoulder before stepping into his office and shutting the door behind her.

Before he said anything, she threw herself at him and kissed him, plastering her body against his. By the time what had happened registered, she had stepped away quickly. "I'm sorry." She sniffled and turned away from him. "I shouldn't have…" She glanced back at him and he was left to just frown as she rushed from the room.

Shit, he thought. What the hell was that? He shook it off, knowing that a lot of brides had the jitters before their wedding. The kiss was quite innocent. She'd barely hit his lips and had gotten most of his cheek instead. If he didn't know better… he stilled. Shit, there was no way she was a virgin kisser, was there? He sat down slowly as a knock sounded on his door.

"Come in," he called out, hoping that it wouldn't be the bride again.

When Bella walked in, his entire attitude changed. She was like a fresh breath of air in his otherwise smoggy day.

"Hi." He smiled easily at her.

"Hi." She moved in when he motioned her to sit down. She glanced back towards the door. "Is everything okay?"

His eyebrows shot up. "Yes, why wouldn't it be?"

"It's just… there was a woman rushing out of here, crying. Is she one of your employees?"

He sighed and stood up to move around the desk. "No, she's the bride-to-be."

"Oh?" Bella glanced back at the closed door as if she were thinking.

"She rushed in here and kissed me." He groaned as he sat on the edge of his desk.

"Oh?" Bella turned back towards him, then slowly crossed her arms over her chest. "Is there something you want to tell me?"

He laughed and then walked over and wrapped his arms around her. "No, trust me. It was as much a shock to me as it is to you. She just came to the resort earlier this morning. I think I've said all of two words to her." He frowned down at Bella. "Her soon-to-be husband on the other hand." He took in a deep breath. "I'd like to take him out back and…" He closed his eyes. "The man's an ass and easily twice the girl's age."

"Girl?" Bella chuckled. "What was she? Twenty-one? Twenty-two?"

"Yeah." He frowned at her and her eyes narrowed up at him.

"Exactly how old do you think I am?" Before he could

answer, she held up her hand. "No, don't answer that." She chuckled. "Did you set her straight? Is that why she was crying?"

"I think I only got out a handful of words before she kissed me. Then she ran off." He glanced towards the door.

"Poor girl, she must be confused. Getting married is scary." She followed his gaze towards the door.

"Not if it's with the right person," he said. She turned back to him, her eyebrows up slightly. "I mean, take a look at your brother and Sarah." He shrugged and dropped his arms from around her.

"Right." She bit her bottom lip as he moved around and sat back down behind his desk.

"I was just finishing up here. How about we head into town and grab some dinner?" he asked.

Her smile returned. "That sounds wonderful. I've been jonesing for some of Ed's pizza."

He chuckled and nodded. "Give me half an hour and I'll meet you out front."

"I'll head upstairs and change." She moved around the desk and laid her lips softly over his. Just before she moved away, he took her face and held her still, letting his lips linger over hers. He enjoyed the softness of her, the taste of her, until his desire built, and he pulled away, knowing if he didn't, he'd want to have her again, right here, right now.

"See you soon." He turned away from her and back to his computer.

CHAPTER THIRTEEN

*B*ella's knees were weak as she left Calvin's office. It took several deep breaths and the walk back up to her room to steady herself after that kiss.

She couldn't deny the bout of jealousy that had hit her when she'd seen the pretty blonde rushing from Calvin's office.

After all, they hadn't made any commitments to each other. As far as she knew, it could have very well just been a one-night deal. She'd never had one before and didn't think Calvin thought of it as such, but she couldn't be sure until she'd talked to him.

But after that kiss… she knew there was more between them. Grabbing a rain jacket, she checked her messages and then freshened up her makeup. Her hair would be a total loss since it was still lightly raining outside.

She glanced down at her watch and figured she had another fifteen minutes and spent the time walking around the room like she was nervously awaiting her first date.

This was ridiculous. It was Calvin. She'd slept with him last night. Why was she nervous? Then it hit her. This was their first date. It somehow meant more to her than he'd suggested they head into town instead of just eating dinner in the dining room downstairs.

He wanted to be seen with her in town.

She did a happy little booty dance and then spent the next few minutes gliding on air as she thought about spending the evening with him. Would he bring her back to his place? That thought stopped her and she rushed to change her smaller purse to a larger one and stuffed some necessities in it just in case.

By the time she'd collected the items, she needed to rush down the stairs so she wouldn't be late meeting him. He was already standing in the lobby holding a large black umbrella as he talked to the man behind the front counter.

When he spotted her, he turned away from the man and smiled at her. "Ready?" he asked, wrapping his arm around her.

"Yes." She sighed at the feeling of his arm around her.

When they stepped out on the front porch, they almost bumped into the pretty blonde woman and an older woman.

"Sorry," Calvin said, trying to step out of the duo's way.

The look both women gave her as they walked past them had Bella holding in a chuckle. As they walked down the pathway towards the docks, she leaned closer to Calvin to be under the cover of the umbrella.

"I'm not sure I am going to survive the attack that just happened," she joked.

"Attack?" His steps faltered.

"Back there." She motioned towards the building.

When he shook his head, she continued. "I don't think it's just the bride that has a thing for you. The other woman was obviously upset that you had your arm around me."

"What?" He stopped at the end of the dock and looked down at her.

"Relax." She giggled and leaned up on her toes and placed a kiss on his lips. "I think they got the hint that you're taken."

He smiled down at her. "Am I?"

She wrapped her arms around him a little more. "If you want to be."

He bent his head down and kissed her slowly, running his lips over hers and making her knees melt. "I do," he said when he pulled back. "We'd better get going or the ferry will take off without us." He nodded towards the boat.

Since it was still raining, most of the employees that were leaving the island for the night huddled inside.

They stood up in the captain's cabin. JT had spotted them crowding onto the ferry and waved them up to ride with him.

"What are you two up to tonight?" he'd asked them.

"Heading into town for some pizza," Calvin had answered easily.

JT glanced between them. "I take it Ben knows?"

Bella sighed loudly. "I do not need approval from my brother on whom I see."

JT chuckled. "Sure, you don't. It's just…" He turned to look over at her. "Don't get me in trouble again."

Bella touched his arm. "He knows that this"—she glanced to Calvin— "is none of his business."

"Besides," Calvin broke in, "Ben's already loosened my jaw for it. Before he gave me his word that it was none of his business."

JT nodded. "Fine." He turned back to her. "If you need a ride back…"

"She won't," Calvin added. Then he turned to her. "I mean, if Bella wants to come back to the resort tonight, I'll bring her myself."

"Fine with me," JT added as he maneuvered the ferry into the dock. "Have a good night. I'm heading home for some dinner myself." He smiled. "We'll have to get together soon so you can see the kids."

"I'd love it," Bella replied.

"Emma's been anxious to meet you."

"Me too," she agreed and remembered suddenly that JT was married to Emma Wilder. Now Emma Thomas. The actress. The woman had played the lead in both of the movies adapted from JT's books. The last one had been full of action, aliens, and Emma kicking some serious butt.

That was before she'd gotten pregnant with their twins. But JT had mentioned that he was working on another sequel. Bella was dying to know if Emma would play the infamous Hannah Rodgers again.

As they stepped off the docks, the sky cleared for a few moments, allowing them to stroll down the street and make their way towards the pizzeria.

The place was packed with families enjoying dinner. She knew a lot more people in town than she'd remembered and enjoyed catching up with a few as they waited for a table to be cleared.

Calvin chatted with a few people she assumed were employees upon hearing parts of their conversation. By the time they were seated at a table near the bar area, she was starving. She'd skipped out on lunch, since she'd buried herself in her work, fine-tuning her latest song, "Just One Night."

When their breadsticks and drinks were delivered, she dug in as they chatted about the town and the people they'd run into.

"What did you do before this?" she asked him after they ordered their pizza.

He shrugged and looked uncomfortable. "This and that."

"Which means?" She chuckled. "I know Sarah and Ben asked you to come in after Lilly had Alex."

"Right," he agreed, reaching for another breadstick. "I was working in Boston."

"For?" she asked, leaning her elbow on the table and watching him.

"A law firm, one I was happy to leave."

"Okay, before that? Ben mentioned something about job jumping before you settled here."

He nodded. "I did. More jobs than I can count or care to revisit. What about you? Did you always want to sing?"

She laughed and relaxed back. "No, when I was ten years old, I wanted to be a superhero. But my parents were quick to dash those hopes. Then I wanted to be a scientist."

"What happened to that dream?"

She shrugged. "I flunked out of biology class."

He chuckled. "So, you turned to music?"

She nodded. "I was good at it and I'd been in choir most of my life." She frowned slightly. "It was funny, my parents were completely fine with me signing, until I told them I wanted to do it for a living."

He reached over and took her hand in his. "Some parents will never be satisfied, no matter what their children do."

"What about your parents?" She watched his eyes and noticed the sadness behind them.

"They have their reasons to be unsatisfied with me. None of them have anything to do with my job." He glanced around the restaurant, avoiding her eyes.

"I won't press you, but if you want to tell me, I'd love to hear more." She took a sip of her wine.

He waited for a moment and she could tell that he was thinking about opening up to her. "For as long as I can remember, every choice I've made seemed to go against their direct wishes." He took a drink of his beer. "After school, things just got worse. That's when I decided to stop trying to please them."

"Where do they live?" she asked.

"New York. Another reason they're upset at me." His voice changed. "Calvin, everyone knows there are more opportunities in one block of the city than there are in the entire state of Maine."

"Your mother?" she guessed.

He nodded. "Dad agrees with everything she says. Always." He rolled his eyes. "Honestly, I don't think my father has a spine of his own, except when it comes to telling his son how disappointed he is in him."

"It can't be all that bad. Even though our parents have voiced their agitation at my career choice, underneath they're proud. Ben caught them bragging about me at the last holiday party he attended of theirs." She smiled remembering her brother's call when he'd told her what her parents had told their closest friends.

"My parents are nothing like yours. I've met your folks and they seem like saints compared to Tammy and Adam Winters."

She frowned down into her wine. "You have a brother?"

He nodded slowly. "James. He's closer to your age..." Her eyebrows shot up as she dared him to mention the handful of years between them. Wisely, he didn't mention it. "He's attending the college my parents told him to, heading towards a career they wanted for him."

"So, he's the perfect child?" She leaned on the table. "You know, growing up, my parents constantly compared me to Ben. Even though they complained about everything to his face, behind his back they used him as a mold for me to fit in. I was constantly asked why I couldn't be more like Ben."

He nodded. "Seeing as I'm the oldest... that wasn't really an issue until..." He stopped and glanced off, then shook his head and took another drink of his beer. So much pain filled his eyes, and she almost reached for his hand. But just then, their pizza arrived, breaking into their conversation.

Taking the first bite into the pizza was like returning to a place she loved. She couldn't help the low moan as her eyes slid closed with pleasure. When her eyes opened again, she realized Calvin was watching her and laughed. "Sorry, it's just… orgasmic."

He smiled. "Yes, it is."

The tone in his voice hinted that he wasn't talking about the pizza, since he'd yet to take a bite. When he leaned closer, he lowered his voice.

"Tell me you're okay with staying with me tonight." His eyes searched hers.

She swallowed and nodded. "I'd planned to."

His smile was instant, and he reached for his slice. "How quickly can we eat?"

She laughed. "Don't rush me." She waved her pizza. "I'm enjoying myself. You can't rush pleasure."

"Oh god." He groaned quietly then took a bite of the pizza.

CHAPTER FOURTEEN

He didn't think he could make the short trip to his house from Ed's. His eyes had been glued to Bella the entire time at the restaurant. He watched as her tongue slid across her bottom lip, licking up the red sauce that had dripped there, and imagined it running across his skin.

The soft moans that emanated from her reminded him of the sounds she'd made the night before when he'd been above her, pleasing her. He wanted his hands on her again. He wanted to taste her skin, to lap her sweet taste up.

It had been too long since he'd been with someone and now that he'd opened the floodgates, it would be hard to close them again. And because it was Bella, his desire was doubled.

He remembered the first time he'd felt lust towards her. It was a photo of Ben's at school. She must have been in her early teens, after the summer in Mexico.

She was wearing light pink leotards on point as she held an almost impossible position in front of a mirror. Her long hair was tied in a tight bun at the nape of her neck as she focused on a point off-screen.

He'd never imagined he'd be so turned on by ballet but seeing her each day as he shared a dorm room with Ben had been like a drug. Over the years the pictures changed as Bella grew. So had his desire for her.

Until he'd seen her walking up the dock, he'd figured he had it under control. Then she'd kissed him, and his world had turned upside down.

They walked huddled together under his umbrella. The three blocks to his house had never seemed as long as they did now.

He finally unlocked his back door and helped her remove her jacket as they stepped into his mudroom. His hands shook as he removed his own.

When he turned to her, she was watching him, and he knew that he couldn't wait another moment.

Pulling her into his arms, his mouth found hers and he felt her tremble in his hold. Or maybe that was him shaking?

The kiss deepened as he pushed her up against the hallway wall. Her hands worked the buttons on his shirt. When she pushed it off his shoulders, she raked her fingernails lightly over his exposed skin, sending waves of goosebumps to raise everywhere on him.

Then it was his turn as he pulled the sweater over her head and smiled down at the pink silk bra she wore underneath. He bent and ran his mouth over it as he lifted her into his arms. Her legs wrapped around his hips.

He walked them quickly into his living room and made it only as far as the sofa before she reached for his belt. Laughing, he turned a little and sat down while she settled on his lap, still trying to remove his belt.

"Easy," he warned as she nipped at his neck.

"No, I can't wait. Let's go fast." She looked into his eyes. "I want this."

He swallowed and felt his desire bubble as she removed his belt and reached for the button of his slacks.

His hands reached and pulled her jeans loose then stood them back up as they both pulled the rest of their clothes off quickly.

When they stood in front of each other, their breathing labored from moving so quickly, he ran his eyes over her. He didn't want to go slow either. He doubted he'd even be able to at this moment. His desire had spiked the moment he'd seen the matching pink silk she wore under her jeans.

"Did you wear these for me?" he asked as he ran a finger over the elastic holding them low on her hips. He played with the soft skin just above the underwear.

"Yes." She groaned and sucked her bottom lip between her teeth.

"My god." He reached over and once again lifted her into his arms. This time when she wrapped her legs around his hips, he moved until he could place her on the corner of his bar top. Pushing his barstools aside, he stood between her legs and kissed her until he knew he couldn't wait any longer. His fingers had found her under the silk and played with her until she'd ground her hips against him and tightened her legs around his waist.

"Cal," she groaned. "I can't wait." She moaned against his neck.

"Just a while longer," he begged and for a split second forgot where he'd put his condoms. Remembering they were upstairs in his nightstand, he reached to pick her up again, only to have her stop him.

"No, here," she begged.

"My condoms are upstairs."

"My purse." She leaned over and reached to where she'd

tossed her purse on the bar top. She dug in the massive bag and came back with a row of the silver packages. He smiled.

"Thank god," he growled out and took one.

After sheathing himself, he reached over and slowly pulled the pink silk down her legs, placing a kiss on her knee as he bent down to remove the material from her. Leaning up, he took one of her legs and tucked it close to his chest as he moved between her thighs again.

She pulled him closer and kissed him as he plunged into her. If he believed he'd lost control earlier, just feeling her wrapped around him left no doubt.

Their movements were frantic, but the fact that they moved together, pleasing one another, was all that mattered. He had never lost control like he was with her. He couldn't even think as she locked her feet behind him and arched into his movements.

When he heard her cry out his name, he knew he wanted to spend the rest of the night pleasing her.

It was an hour before they finally made it upstairs to his bedroom. She'd pulled on his work shirt, leaving the top four buttons undone. She looked so damn sexy that when they got upstairs, he took his time removing the shirt and pleasing her by licking every inch of her soft skin.

Falling asleep with Bella in his arms was indescribable to him. He'd never had a woman stay over at this house before.

When he'd lived in Boston, he'd had a couple of short-term relationships, but he hadn't officially dated anyone since he'd moved into town. He'd had a few dates, but none of them had gone anywhere outside a few dinners or group events with Ben and the rest of his friends. This was the first time he'd brought a woman over to this house.

He knew that meant something. Hell, to be honest, he'd known before Ben had clocked him that Bella meant some-thing to him. He'd sensed it even before touching her.

Glancing down at her dark hair fanning out over his pillow, he wondered if this was just a casual deal to her. The way she'd talked about Michael and what had happened between them made him think that wasn't so. But it was obvious after that first night that she had no qualms about taking a casual lover.

Could he mean something more to her too? Was that why she'd agreed to spend the night with him?

Then his mind turned to the conversation they'd had during dinner. He knew there were things he had to tell her. Confessions he needed to make and other things he had to clear up if they were going to move forward with any kind of relationship.

When his mind finally shut down, he knew that he'd pay for the late hour the following day. When his alarm went off, he wished he didn't have to be there for the Wright and Stafford rehearsal party.

Bella groaned, and he rolled over and wrapped his arms around her. "Go back to bed. Stay as long as you want and catch the ferry back when you want."

"No." She sighed and leaned up to trail her mouth over his jaw. "You need a shave." She chuckled, running her hands over his face. "If you have time…" She started moving against him. He'd woken up hard from the way her soft scent had surrounded him, but now he felt himself growing even harder. "I can help you."

He groaned. "For the first time in years"—he bent down and ran his mouth over her neck— "I just may be late to work."

She sighed and arched. "You did say you had your boat." She purred as his fingers found her, wet and ready for him.

They stepped onto the docks over an hour later, loaded down with a bag of muffins and coffee from the local bakery.

He was going to be only a few minutes late and had already called ahead to the resort to let them know.

Stopping beside his boat, he was jerked to a stop when Bella tugged on his arm. He glanced back at her in question.

"This is yours?" She frowned at his sailboat.

He chuckled. "Yes, I thought you knew." He shrugged. "It's the reason your brother and his friends always include me. I'm the only one with a boat big enough to accommodate all of us."

"Why didn't you tell me the other day that this was yours?" she asked as he helped her step onto the deck.

"The *Dame* and I go back a few years." He chuckled. "She was my first buy when I got a full-time job. Well, after the house." He shrugged. "But she was the most important." He unhooked them from his slip at the dock. "Actually, your brother pays for my slip." He nodded towards the spot as he turned on the motor, after making sure she was sitting down next to him. "In exchange for the freedom to take her out whenever he wants." He leaned closer to her and added. "I would let him for a case a beer a month, but…" He shrugged. "Ben insists."

"Now I feel… bad. You know, getting sick." She motioned to the cabin below them.

"You're not going to be sick now, are you?" He frowned down at her.

"No, I think it was just a one-time deal. There was a lot of stress…" She sighed and took another sip of her coffee.

He nodded in agreement. "Do you feel well enough to eat?" he asked as they started out of the dock area. Missing the morning ferry had a few perks, such as being able to be alone with her for breakfast.

"I hope so. I'm starved." She laughed over at him.

"Good." He turned the motor off and moved over towards her.

"Can you just leave us floating like this?" she asked as she glanced around, a worried look on her face.

He chuckled. "Do you see any other boats?"

She shook her head no. "But aren't there some sort of… routes or rules you have to follow?"

"Like a flight plan?" He chuckled and pulled out a bottle of orange juice and handed it to her.

Bella shrugged. "Okay, so I guess boating isn't as regulated as driving or flying."

"Other than a handful of rules, like those in a no-wake zone, it's pretty much an open field out here." He bit into his muffin.

She relaxed back and for the next few minutes they enjoyed their breakfast as the sun continued to rise and heat them.

"You have a big party today?" she asked.

"Yes," he said, finishing off the muffin and swallowing the last of his juice. "I'm going to be busy for the next few days. Until after the wedding Saturday morning."

"I ran into the groom-to-be after I left your office yesterday," Bella said after he started the motor again. She'd moved to stand beside him. When she swayed and almost toppled over, he reached around and wrapped his arms around her, tucking her between him and the massive wheel.

He felt her sigh against him.

"And?" he asked, enjoying her softness against him.

"I agree with your assessment. I can't see why the bride doesn't see through his fake charm. He was standing in the door to his room, berating the waiter who had brought up his dinner."

"Which one?" He frowned.

Bella thought about it. "Ed?" She tilted her head. "I think that was his name."

"Eddie." He nodded. "Is there anything I should know in particular? What did Eddie do to instigate it?"

She turned to look over her shoulder at him. "I don't think he did anything." Cal slowed down as they pulled into the dock at the resort. "Whatever he did, I doubt it deserved the reaming he got."

"Right." He shifted. "Wanna help me tie this off?"

She bit her bottom lip in question. "What do I have to do?"

He smiled. "Toss a rope."

She laughed. "Then I'm game."

For the next few minutes, he instructed her on how to help until his boat sat secured in one of the slips. He couldn't count how many times he'd boated to work over the last few years. Once, when JT had taken the ferry in for a new paint job, he'd used it to shuttle most of the employees to work for an entire week.

He pulled Bella to a stop at the end of the dock, figuring they should say their goodbyes in private.

"I don't know when I'll have time to see you today." He brushed a strand of her dark hair away from her face, wishing they could spend the entire day together.

"That's okay." She smiled. "I have a few things I wanted to do." She leaned up on her toes and kissed him.

"If you need anything," he said when she moved back.

"I'll find you." She smiled up at him and he felt his heart skip at the look she was giving him.

Taking her hand, he walked with her to the main building and, just before stepping into the clearing, he dropped his hand, knowing that their relationship should remain private as much as possible.

CHAPTER FIFTEEN

Bella was floating as she made her way up the stairs. She'd never had a night as wonderful as last night with Calvin.

How was she supposed to focus on anything when her body was still vibrating from what they'd done to each other? What Calvin had done to her.

Her mind was so busy replaying last night that when she stepped into her rooms, the scene didn't register at first. She had to blink a few times before the mess finally sunk in. She stepped back out of the door. She came to a stop when she bumped into a young maid pushing a cart.

"Is everything all right, miss?" the girl said smoothly in a southern accent.

"My… room." She shook her head. "Someone broke into it." She motioned towards the door.

The maid frowned at her, but then stepped past her and gasped as she looked inside. "Are you all right miss?"

Bella nodded. "I… just got back."

"I'll call the manager," the woman said, touching her arm.

"Why don't you come over here and have a seat. You're very pale."

Bella allowed the woman to drag her to a settee underneath a wide window.

She didn't know how long it took Calvin to get there, only that it seemed like he was there in a blink of an eye. He knelt in front of her, taking her hands in his.

"Are you okay?" he asked, concern flooding his eyes.

She nodded. "Someone broke into my rooms. They… destroyed everything." She felt her eyes start to burn.

She wasn't so concerned about the things she'd seen broken or thrown around the space, but for the intrusion into her privacy. Then she froze at remembering several of the threats she'd received. Did this have anything to do with Michael? Would he send someone out here to scare her? Could he stoop this low?

She realized Calvin had been talking to her and cleared her thoughts so she could hear him finish.

"…stay here." He started to stand up.

"Wait." She took his hands, holding him still. "What if they're still in there?"

"I think we're safe." He smiled at her. "I'll be right back." He squeezed her hand lightly, then stood and nodded to the maid. "Linda's going to stay with you."

Bella glanced over to the maid, who moved over and sat next to her. Then she turned and watched Calvin disappear into her rooms. She held her breath, trying to listen down the hallway for any signs of a struggle.

It seemed to take forever and when he finally stepped out again, she relaxed. "I've called the police," he said, avoiding her eyes as he motioned for Linda. "Let's try to keep everyone clear of this floor until the police are done. Then we'll need everyone up here to help clean the mess." He sighed and Bella noticed a frustrated look in his eyes. "We'll need a few things replaced in there before we let anyone stay in those rooms again."

Bella swallowed at the memory of the destruction she'd seen.

"Hey, why don't you let me take you on down to the dining hall? You can sit and have a cup of coffee and some of Adam's coffee bread while we wait for the police to arrive."

She took several deep breaths. "Did they destroy any of my things?" Before he opened his mouth to say anything, she knew the answer. "How bad?"

He sighed. "Your clothes are destroyed… well, most of them." He had an odd look, but then he shook his head. "I'm afraid your iPad and laptop are toast."

She closed her eyes and groaned.

"Come on." He pulled her up into his arms. "Linda, I'm walking her downstairs. Make sure everyone steers clear of this floor until I get back."

Linda nodded as Calvin led her towards the stairs.

"Cal, was there anything else?" she asked, biting her lip. If this was a simple break-in, they would have stolen her things instead of destroying them.

He stopped on the landing and looked down at her. Again, she could see that he wanted to tell her something.

"Someone used your lipstick to write a message on the wall." He was running his hands up and down her arms, warming her. Suddenly, she realized she was freezing.

"What did it say?" she asked. When he opened his mouth, she could tell he was going to make an excuse not to tell her, so she gave him a look that said, don't even try to hide it from me. It must have done the trick because he sighed and then answered.

"You'll never hide from me," he said in a deep voice laced with anger. "Do you think this was Himes?"

The words had her vibrating with fear, and she shivered.

Calvin pulled her into a hug. She closed her eyes and rested her forehead on Calvin's shoulder.

"I don't know," she said finally with a sigh. "I'm not sure of anything right now."

Could Michael be so out of control? After all, he hadn't really shown that much interest in her. Sure, he'd acted like they'd been seeing one another a lot longer than they had. As if they were romantically involved beyond the three casual dates.

She had done some research, and she understood that most stalkers didn't need encouragement to go off the deep end. If Michael was behind all this, then those three dates were all it took in his mind to warrant the crazy.

She had a growing ache that spread throughout her entire body and knew that it was the weariness of the last few months seeping in.

"Come on." He pulled her up to her feet, his arms still wrapped around her. "Let's head down and get you something warm to drink."

She followed him down the stairs. Actually, she allowed him to drag her down there since she wasn't really feeling in control of anything anymore.

He set her in a booth in the back corner, away from the large wedding group that filled the main part of the dining room.

A cup was shoved in her hands and only after she'd taken a sip did she realize that it was hot chocolate instead of coffee. The sweetness was welcomed. A plate of coffee cake was set in front of her just as Calvin disappeared back up the stairs. She nibbled on it. It was wonderful, so she focused on eating instead of the quick glimpse that she'd had of her rooms.

When Calvin returned, her mug and plate were empty, and she was on her phone with her agent. The sugar had allowed her fears to dissipate, which made room for her anger to bubble.

"I don't care how it will look. I want a restraining order filed by the end of the day." She glanced up as Calvin sat across from her, his eyes narrowing at her words.

"I doubt it's going to do anything, really," Maggie was saying in her ear, "but I thought we should do it after you started receiving those emails."

Bella sighed and avoided Calvin's eyes as she looked out over the green lawn. There wasn't a single cloud in the sky today. The rains had turned everything super clean outside, and Bella could just imagine how the soft breeze smelled of saltwater and grass.

"Well, we're doing it now. I think I'm ready for that interview."

"Really?" Maggie's voice spiked slightly. "Do you think you're in the right state of mind?"

"Who cares." She shifted her phone to her other ear. "I'm the victim here, and it's about time the public knew it. The man is powerful in Hollywood, and I won't be pushed around and afraid for the rest of my life."

"I'll set it all up," Maggie confirmed. "I'm really sorry about your things. Will you be returning to California soon then?"

Bella's eyes moved over to Calvin, and she thought about jumping on a plane to LA and frowned. "No," she answered quickly. "Not yet."

"Are you sure? It's obvious his reach is wide. It's not like you're any safer there than here."

"I am." She smiled at Cal, who smiled back. She could tell he couldn't hear what Maggie was saying. "I'll call you later tonight when I know where I'll be."

"You'll be at my place," Calvin broke in.

"Was that your brother?" Maggie asked.

"No," she said into the phone. "I'll... text you the address where I'm staying," she said before hanging up.

"No?" Calvin asked, tilting his head slightly.

"That no was for Maggie, not for you." She played with her napkin. "I don't want to be a burden on you."

He chuckled. "You're not." His hand closed over hers. "I promised your brother I'd watch out for you."

She felt her heart sink a little at the thought that she was just a promise between friends.

"Besides," he added with a smile, "I like having you in my bed."

She smiled and relaxed slightly, then glanced towards the stairs. "My things?"

"I'm having what few clothes of yours survived cleaned and packed up for you. They should be ready for us later." He glanced around. "If you want, I can get you another room for a few hours."

She shook her head, not enjoying the thought of being alone in a hotel room for a few hours, even though she was feeling a little tired after the rush of the emotions.

"My office has a sofa," he suggested.

"That sounds nice." Then she asked the dreaded question. "Did my guitar survive?"

He shook his head slightly and slid out of the booth to pull her up into his arms. "No, I'm sorry."

"It's okay." She sighed into his arms.

"Come on." He stepped back. "I'll take you up to my office. You can rest."

Three hours later, Calvin woke her from the nap she hadn't believed she would take. He'd left her sitting in his office and, at first, she'd walked around the space, trying to come up with her next move. Then she'd sat down and closed her eyes for just a moment, since her head was throbbing.

"I didn't mean to wake you," he said, sitting beside her on the sofa.

"It's okay." She stretched her arms over her head and rolled her shoulders. Before she could say anything else, he pulled her close and kissed her, making her wish that they could spend a few hours napping together.

"I've got our lunch planned, if you feel like stepping out and enjoying some sunshine," he suggested.

She thought about it and nodded. "That sounds wonderful."

She was surprised when he led her down one of the pathways towards the small beach area. There, on the pebbled shore, lay a large green blanket with a picnic lunch ready for them. She assumed the food was still tucked in the basket sitting off to the side. There was even a bottle of wine chilling in a bucket.

"Wow." She glanced around. "You did all this? What if someone else had come along first?"

He chuckled and helped her sit down. "Then we'd eat up in the dining room instead." He sat down and opened the wine. He poured her a glass and handed it to her. Then he opened the basket and started laying out the food.

"It's one of the services we offer." He motioned towards the picnic. "I didn't do anything except put in the order," he admitted with a smile.

"You poured the wine," she pointed out.

He laughed. "I did." He handed her a container filled with lemon herb chicken.

"I've never had a picnic on the beach before," she admitted after her plate was full.

"You haven't?" He tilted his head. "I guess this is my first time too. I've brought many lunches out here for some quiet time, but I don't think that counts."

She shook her head and agreed. "No, it doesn't."

"To firsts... together." He held up his glass of soda and she tipped her glass of wine against it.

She was thankful that Calvin went out of his way to make the lunch conversation light and fun. She laughed and flirted with him while enjoying the sun and the fresh sea air.

When he glanced down at his phone after it chimed, he frowned over at her. "And that's my lunch break."

She sighed, not wanting to leave the warmth of the beach.

"Feel free to stick around." He motioned to the now crowded beach. There were more than a dozen people lounging around or swimming in the water. A few others had picnics like theirs.

"I think I will. At least for a while." She sighed and relaxed back, wishing for her own swimsuit. Then she glanced sideways at him. "Did my swimsuit survive?"

He shrugged as he dusted off his work slacks. "I didn't really take stock."

She nodded. "If not, Serenity's has some really cute ones I saw in there the other day."

He chuckled and then bent down to kiss her. "I'll come find you after the party. It starts in an hour."

She held him down and kissed him again. "I may just nap here now," she admitted.

He chuckled. "You are on vacation."

"Right," she admitted as he pulled away.

"If you need me." He wiggled his phone.

"Thanks, for the lunch and... for everything," she said. He nodded and she watched him disappear back down the pathway.

She lay around enjoying the sun until she grew thirsty. A resort worker had come and hauled the remains of the picnic away shortly after Calvin had left. She noticed a few of them standing around the beach, most likely on guard, watching out for her. Thanks to Calvin.

Dusting her jeans off, she made her way away from the beach. She had just stepped onto the pathway when she heard an argument. She thought about turning back and finding another way to the pool bar area.

She stopped when she heard the slap. There was no mistaking the sound of skin on skin followed by a woman's slight cry of pain. Rushing forward, she went on the defense as all thoughts of her own safety fled her mind.

CHAPTER SIXTEEN

Calvin remained so busy after lunch that by the time the rehearsal party rolled around, he hadn't had any free time to think about Bella again.

The finishing touches were in place as the wedding party started arriving. Everyone was standing around waiting for the groom and bride to arrive when the bride's mother rushed over to him.

"What have you done?" she hissed at him as she tugged his arm, trying to get him away from the group of family members he'd been chatting with.

"Is there a problem, Miss Wright?" he asked, stepping aside so their conversation wouldn't be heard.

"Yess," she hissed again as she glanced around. "You are the problem. I can't believe the lack of professionalism." She shook her head. "Your boss will hear about this."

He waited until she was done. "I'm sorry, if there's anything my staff has…"

The woman laughed sarcastically. "Your employees are not at fault. You are. I'm going to hold you financially responsible for everything."

He shook his head. "I'm sorry, I'm not following you." He looked around and saw Fredrick Stafford heading his way. To say the man looked pissed would have been an understatement.

He waited for the man to stop in front of him, but instead, the guy threw his fist back and swung it at Calvin's head. Thankfully, Calvin had seen the move coming, since the man wasn't in any shape to fight.

Before he could respond, two of his staff members rushed over and, between the three of them, they held the man's arms down to his side as he filled the air with colorful curse words.

"Would one of you like to tell me what this is all about?" he asked when the man ran out of steam. It didn't take long. There was a bead of sweat rolling down the heavy man's face, which had turned a bright red.

"That," Fredrick spat out, "was for sleeping with my virgin bride."

The entire group of family members had all gathered around to watch the show. Everyone gasped at this and glared in his direction, as if already judging him as guilty.

Calvin couldn't help it, he laughed. "This is some sort of joke." He looked around. Catching Kathleen Wright's eyes, he knew that they weren't joking.

"I haven't slept with or, for that matter, done anything with Miss Wright except having a very brief conversation with her yesterday," he responded. Then he remembered how the younger woman had thrown herself at him and frowned.

"See." Fredrick tried to point a beefy hand at him. "It's written all over your face. You can't deny it."

"I can and I am," he said again. "I'm involved with someone else at the moment," he added.

"So? Once a cheater…" someone in the growing crowd

called out.

He glared around and shook his head. "I'm not sure what brought this matter up. If I'm being accused, please tell me, who is it that witnessed this act?" Everyone was silent, so he added. "Now, if we're all settled." He moved closer to Fredrick and lowered his voice. "Have you considered this rumor was started to stop the wedding?"

The man's eyes narrowed, then he turned on Kathleen. "Where is your daughter?"

"She's here." Calvin heard Bella's voice and watched the crowd part as she marched towards them, holding onto Eliza's arm.

The blonde woman was holding an ice pack to her cheek and looking as if she wished she were anywhere else but in the middle of a crowd.

The look on Bella's face had Calvin holding his breath. He'd never seen her so riled up before. She was obviously pissed about something. Standing back, he waited to see what was going on.

"I've called the police," she informed him and turned her body towards the man still being held back by two of the resort's employees.

"Good," the man sneered. "They'll sort this mess out and—"

"Arrest you," Bella finished as she crossed her arms over her chest.

"Me?" Fredrick balked. "For what? He's the one who slept with my virgin bride."

"Virgin…" Bella hissed. "You disgust me." Bella stood closer and Calvin's arms moved to her shoulders, trying to keep her a safe distance from the man. "And no, he didn't. You crossed the line when you hit her." Bella motioned to the woman, who was trying to hide behind them.

A hush fell over the crowd as every eye turned on her

now. She avoided everyone's gaze.

"Is this true?" Kathleen gasped, rushing over to her daughter. The mother gently raised her hand and pulled the ice pack away from Eliza's face. There, on the girl's cheek, was a nasty red mark, clearly in the shape of a hand. Her skin was marred with red lines, as if the blood vessels had burst under her pale skin.

Gasps once again circled amongst the group as stares turned towards Fredrick.

"She's lying," the man screamed out. "It was probably him." He motioned towards Calvin.

"Enough," Calvin barked out. "I will not be dragged into this. I'm in a committed relationship and have not cheated, nor do I have the desire to." He narrowed his eyes and circled the group, waiting for anyone to challenge him. "Now, I suggest we wait until the police get here to deal with this matter instead of throwing around accusations."

"I saw it all," Bella chimed in suddenly. "I was just heading to the pool bar for an iced tea after my picnic at the beach and was around the corner when I heard the slap. I showed up just as he"—she pointed towards Fredrick— "was leaving. I helped Eliza back up from the ground." She motioned to the woman. "She has cuts on her hands and knees as well."

"I guess that settles it," someone in the crowd said. "Guess the wedding's off."

"Thank god," Calvin heard someone else say. Suddenly, the crowd broke up as two Silver Cove police officers arrived.

"What's this all about, Calvin," Brock asked as he stopped by him.

The key players were moved into Calvin's office for privacy. He sat behind his desk, listening to the entire story again as Bella sat in one of his chairs and Eliza cried softly on her mother's shoulder.

"This is all lies," Fredrick barked out when Bella got to the point of witnessing the slap. "To cover up the fact that that man"—he pointed at Calvin again— "slept with my bride."

"You keep saying that," Calvin said easily. "It makes it no truer than before."

Calvin heard Brock chuckle. "Calvin?" Brock shook his head. "No way."

"Why not?" Fredrick asked with a frown.

"Because," Brock started, "everyone in town knows he and Bella…" He stopped talking. "Well, they've just started seeing one another."

"Thank you, Brock," Calvin broke in. "Who started this nasty rumor anyway?" he asked Fredrick, whose eyes moved over to Eliza.

Everyone turned to her. The woman swallowed and then shrugged.

"I met with Fredrick to break things off." She looked down at her hands. "After the other day…" Her eyes moved up to his. "I'm sorry I kissed you."

Fredrick barked out. "See!"

"Shut up," Brock said then turned to Eliza. "Go on."

"Well, I just wanted to know what it was like, to kiss someone I wanted. For once. I decided I didn't want to go ahead with this marriage." She turned to her mother. "I know I promised, but I can't marry someone I don't love. I don't even like him." She motioned toward the man.

"It's okay, sweetie, we'll figure something out." Kathleen sighed and hugged her daughter, who started crying again.

"I swear," she said as she cried, "I haven't slept with anyone. I just told Fredrick I kissed him and had changed my mind about the wedding."

Brock turned towards the man. "Did you hit Eliza?" he asked.

Suddenly, Fredrick's entire demeanor changed. It was like

someone had turned on a switch and he had turned back into Dr. Jekyll. He watched as the guy started oozing charm.

"I think we can all see how she misled me." He chuckled and relaxed. "She led me to believe that he'd taken advantage of my sweet, young, innocent bride. This is all an obvious misunderstanding." He moved to get up, dusting off his slacks and straightening his shirt. When he made a move towards the doorway, Kathleen stood up.

"My daughter wishes to press charges against Fredrick Stafford." She held her hand and pointed at the man who currently had a hand on the doorknob, looking like he was desperately trying to escape.

The man turned and was once again Mr. Hyde. "It's a lie," he screamed, his face turning red. "I never touched the girl."

The yelling started again, and Calvin glanced over at Bella, who looked over at him and then leaned towards him and whispered.

"You never told me your job was so… exciting."

He couldn't help it, he laughed and pulled her into his arms right there.

An hour later, they sat in his office alone. The group had broken up shortly after the police cuffed Fredrick Stafford and hauled him into the local station.

No doubt the guy would post bond and be out before the fingerprint ink could dry, but at least it was all legal and on record. Kathleen had convinced Eliza to sue the man for abuse and emotional turmoil, no doubt seeking to recoup some of the funds they had lost putting on the elaborate show.

The mother and daughter checked out less than ten minutes after the police had left and requested as much of a refund as possible. Calvin assured them that he would have a look at the expenses and refund what they could.

"Come here," he said, wiggling his finger towards Bella.

She smiled and stood up from the chair and slowly made her way across the room towards him. She'd had to tell her story officially once more and had signed a statement before Brock had left.

She didn't stop when she got to him, instead she straddled him and wrapped her arms around his neck.

He pulled her down to a kiss and sighed when he realized just how right it felt.

"I just can't get over that man thinking Eliza was his property." She sighed against his neck as she hugged him. "He kept saying 'my bride,' as if he owned her." She leaned back. "Did he actually say, my innocent virgin bride?"

Calvin thought about it and nodded. "Yes, I believe those were his words."

"That's disgusting. I mean, it sounds like he was paying for a virgin sacrifice." He felt her shiver.

He chuckled. "You watch too many movies."

She shook her head and smiled slightly. "I hope Eliza finds happiness now." Then she leaned back even further, and her smile grew. "Does that mean you have the night off now?"

He laughed and kissed her. "It does," he agreed. "What did you have in mind?"

The last thing he'd expected when he secured the *Dame* back in her slip at the Silver Cove docks was that an hour later he'd be standing in Serenity's Attic holding bags full of clothes Bella had purchased from other stores while he waited for Bella to step out of the dressing room again.

"This isn't what I had in mind," he said softly when she stepped out wearing a soft blue sundress.

"You don't like it?" She twirled, sending the skirt flowing around her. The back had a sexy strap of thin material that crossed her body.

"I like it," he said, his voice going low with desire. "But I had hoped we would skip the shopping."

She chuckled and waved him away as she turned to the mirror to look at her image. The smile on her face told him that she liked the dress herself and he would, no doubt, be carrying it, along with the other three items she'd already decided on, home that night.

"We have time," she said over her shoulder. "Besides, I needed some retail therapy."

He remembered that most of her things had been destroyed that morning and nodded. It really wasn't a hardship, watching her try on sexy outfits or helping her pick out things he liked.

They had stopped at the boutique a few doors down, and he'd helped her pick out all new underwear and bras. She'd been very interested in his opinions, but all he could think about was getting her back to his place after then. He hadn't planned on making two more stops.

"Oh, I like that one," Crystal said. The woman had three more dresses in her hands and set them across the back of a chair near the dressing rooms for Bella to try on. "It sets off your aura nicely."

The woman's eyes went soft and she sighed as she looked between them. "It's so wonderful." She walked over and wrapped an arm around Calvin's waist. "You and my Calvin." She chuckled.

Since he'd met Sarah's mother, the woman had taken to him like a second mother. Well, actually, Crystal was the mother he'd always wished he'd had instead of his own.

"I knew the two of you would be a great pair," Crystal added. "Oh, you need some jasmine." She snapped her fingers and quickly disappeared.

Bella chuckled and turned back to him. "I missed being home." She grabbed up the other dresses, kissed him, then disappeared into the dressing room again.

CHAPTER SEVENTEEN

It was so nice having a different place to sleep. One where someone hadn't broken in. Just the little intrusion was enough to creep her out.

Stepping into Calvin's house again this night was a lot different than the night before. Sure, she felt passion for him bubbling up inside her again, but tonight they were both weighed down by bags of items she had purchased.

Her luggage, filled with her remaining clothes, sat just inside his front door.

"Want me to help you put your stuff away?" he asked, setting some of the bags on his sofa.

She had been dying to ask him how long he expected her to stay. After all, she only had a week left of her planned vacation time.

Her brother and his family were due back tomorrow. They'd heard about the break-in and had cut their trip short.

She'd assumed Calvin had invited her to stay at his place for the night, until she could move over to Ben and Sarah's place.

"That depends," she said after setting down the bags she'd been carrying.

"On?" He moved over to her and wrapped his arms around her waist, pulling her close.

"Your plans," she said under her breath.

"My plans?" he asked, his dark eyebrows slowly going up. She nodded and swallowed at the feeling she got when looking into his eyes. Feeling his body next to hers always caused her breath to catch in her lungs. "Well, currently, I plan on helping you get settled upstairs." He leaned down and brushed his lips across hers. "Then I plan on eating something before taking you to bed and making love to you slowly for the rest of the night."

She closed her eyes on a moan at the thought. "I mean…" She shifted slightly so she could look up at him again. "How long do you plan on me staying with you?"

His smile slipped slightly. "As long as you want." He shrugged. "I've got plenty of room. For your own safety, I plan on you coming to work with me each day so I can keep an eye on you." He frowned even a little more. "Or you'll be hanging out with your brother or Sarah. We've all decided not to let you out of our sight for too long."

She groaned when she remembered the conversation she'd had with her brother. "Right." She nodded. "I didn't know if you expected…" She shook her head and leaned against him further.

"If you want, I'd like you to remain here with me." He used his fingers to raise her chin up until she was looking into his eyes again. "Is that what you're asking?"

She nodded. "I'd like that." She smiled.

"Good. Now that that is settled, let's get your stuff upstairs."

They spent the next hour hanging her clothes in his massive walk-in closet. Over half of the space had been sitting empty except for the empty boxes from when he'd moved in two years ago. He folded them up and took them out to his garage as she hung each of her new items and inspected the other clothes that had been salvaged.

She was thankful that most of her shoes had survived the attack. When she was done, she moved into his bathroom and found an empty drawer to put her toiletry items in.

"Settled?" he asked from the doorway. He'd disappeared about a half an hour ago to head downstairs and make them dinner.

"Yes." She turned to him and looked around. "I don't want to invade…" He stopped her by walking over and kissing her.

"You aren't," he said smoothly. "Don't even think about it. While you are here, treat this like your home. Don't be one of those guests that make it weird." He chuckled. "Okay?"

She nodded. "Okay."

"Good, now come on downstairs. You can set the table while I finish up with dinner." He kissed her again and then pulled her downstairs.

She busied herself setting the table after he showed her where to find everything. She was happy that he didn't treat her like a guest. When she stayed with Ben and Sarah, they had treated her the same way.

It was strange to remember living with her parents. She had always felt like a guest in their home growing up.

The last time she'd visited them, before she'd graduated school, they had put her up in a guest room, since they'd changed her bedroom into a study for her mother. Like her mother needed a study. The woman hadn't held a job Bella's entire life.

"You're deep in thought," Calvin said to her as he set a tray of cheese and crackers on the table.

Taking up one, she shrugged. "Thinking about my parents."

He stilled as his eyes ran over her. "And?"

She shrugged as she chewed, then reached for the glass of wine he'd given her before she'd started setting the table. After taking a sip, she answered.

"I was just thinking how I feel more at home here than I do in my childhood home."

He walked over and wrapped his arms around her. "I know how that feels." He kissed the top of her head. "I'm happy you feel comfortable here." He chuckled. "Everyone feels comfortable here. I think it's the place." He glanced around.

She laughed. "No, it's the company."

He smiled down at her. "Come on, dinner's ready." He stepped back and then pulled out a chair for her.

She sat as he carried out a tray of grilled chicken covered in a honey barbeque sauce sitting on rice and vegetables. The meal looked amazing.

"Wow, this looks great," she said as he set it in the middle of the table, then took a seat next to her.

"Don't get too excited. This is one of the five meals I know how to make." He wiggled his eyebrows causing her to laugh.

"That's better than the three I know." She held up her fingers. "Grilled cheese, mac and cheese, and—my all-time favorite—carryout."

He shook his head. "I remember living in the city, a carryout restaurant on every corner. Where else could you have Chinese one night and Middle Eastern food the next?" He sighed. "Those were the days. I had Adam teach me a few basic meals so I could survive. Not that we don't have some good choices in town."

"I get it. Sometimes you just want a quiet meal at home." She glanced around.

Last night, she had been too busy with him to really get a good look at the home.

A row of windows faced off towards the water, letting streaks of bright colors from the sunset stream into the dining room and living room. The kitchen was on the far end of the main floor, closest to the road. The stairs sat directly in the middle of the home and went up to the three bedrooms. The master had the same view overlooking the water.

She'd peeked her head into the other rooms while he'd been downstairs. He'd turned one into an office and the other was a guest bedroom.

Narrow stairs led up to the third floor. She didn't know what was up there since she didn't want to snoop. Nor had she been downstairs to the basement or the garage.

"You got quiet." He motioned with his fork.

"I was just thinking about this place. You know, when I got my first record deal, I rented a small place downtown." She laughed. "I'm still there." She shook her head and took another bite.

"City living is different. This is the first place I put down roots." He motioned around. "Sarah and Lilly took over with the decorations. I gave them input here or there, but for the most part…" He tilted his head as he looked at the painting hanging over his fireplace. She followed his gaze and smiled. "I like everything they chose."

"Is that an Allison Jordan painting?" she asked, wanting to get up and inspect the painting of a small crisp white dingy floating in dark waters.

"It is." He smiled. "My one contribution. I bought it a few years back at an auction." He sighed. "I've always admired great art."

"Me too." She'd finished her meal, so she set her fork down and crossed the room. She could just get lost in the scene. Why was the small craft so far out in the deep water? Was there someone lying in the bow of the boat? Resting or suffering?

Suddenly, she realized she was the small boat. Floating in a sea of uncertainty, alone. Her eyes stung as tears threatened to surface. How had she allowed her life to get to this place?

When she'd lived with Ben and Sarah after moving in with them in high school, she'd turned things around. She'd no longer felt lonely as she had under her parents' rule.

Ben and Sarah had shown her what a family should be. Then she'd followed her dream out west and lost that insight into what she could have. What she could be.

Not that she didn't like her singing career. She just hated being in LA amongst all the pretentious people in their never-ending battle to be on top.

When the threats had started, the first thing she'd thought of was to run home to her brother and Sarah. Now, she was beginning to think that she'd dug herself in such a deep hole, there was no place she could go to escape the clutches of the madman.

She jumped slightly when Calvin's hands rested on her shoulder.

"I love that her paintings leave so much to your imagination." He sighed as he wrapped his arms around her. He turned her towards him and frowned down at her. "Hey, are you okay?"

She nodded and laid her head against his shoulder. "I guess it's just getting to me. The intrusion." She closed her eyes and let his sexy scent consume her.

"I'm sorry," he said into her hair. "I don't know what it's like to have my things destroyed. I'm here." He ran his hands up and down her back.

"It's not about the things." She leaned back slightly and

looked up into his eyes. She knew she could trust him as much as she trusted her brother and Sarah.

"It's me," she said pointing to the boat. He waited, quietly, until she continued. "I'm the dingy floating out in the rough ocean. With no set path. No help in sight." She closed her eyes as tears slid down her cheeks. "The waves crashing against me, tossing me every direction except for the one I want to go."

His arms tightened around her. "You aren't alone." He kissed the top of her head. "I'm here. Ben and Sarah are here for you."

She nodded. "Here." She pulled back and looked up at him. "Not in LA."

He gently reached up and wiped the tears from her face. "Then why go back?"

She'd been asking herself that same question since stepping off the ferry at the resort. The only thing left for her in California were items she could easily have shipped back here or replaced.

Sure, she had a few commitments. She had to go in at the end of the month to finish her next album, and for some photo shoots, music videos, and other promotional appearances. But the more she thought it through, the more she realized she could travel across the country for those events.

"You're right." She sighed and leaned up to kiss him.

He turned her slightly. "Don't you see it?" He nodded to the painting. "The hope? After all, that's what this piece is called. Hope."

She shook her head, but then she stilled and tilted her head. There, in the distance of the painting off to the far right of the dingy, was a single ray of sunshine shining on a green shoreline. The dingy was even pointing in the right direction, the currents in the dark water moving towards the landmass.

Since she had already opened up a little, she figured she better tell him the rest. Moving over to the sofa, she sat down and waited until he sat beside her.

"I've been getting emails and calls…" She took a deep breath.

"You told me…" When she shook her head, he grew silent. "Okay," he said slowly.

"Threats. Credible ones. At least the police think they are. Enough that they suggested I take some time away. To stay someplace safe."

He waited for her to say more, but she didn't know what to say. Instead, she pulled out her phone and opened her messages and showed him. She sat silently beside him while he read the disturbing messages, more than a dozen of them.

Messages about someone's desire to chop her up. To tear her to pieces. To listen to her scream as they drained the blood from her body.

"I feel sick." He closed his eyes and handed her back her phone. "Why didn't you tell us about these earlier?"

"Because the police are handling it." She shrugged and set her phone down on the coffee table. "They have a task force… or whatever, to try to track down whoever sent them. Since they officially crossed the line into…" She shook her head and didn't want to say the words. "Disturbing."

"Disturbing?" He stood up suddenly and paced in front of the fireplace. "That doesn't come close to what those messages are." He turned suddenly. "Psychopathic does." He moved back to her. "You need a full force of security on you." He glanced around the house.

She could see fear and concern as he looked around his safe space suddenly as if they were out in the open in the middle of a war.

"Calvin." She stood up and wrapped her arms around him. "I can't hide forever." She took his face into her hands and leaned up to kiss him. "The police have assured me that they will catch whoever sent these."

"Oh my god." He stilled even further. "Do you think whoever broke into your rooms last night and cut your things up with garden shears…"

To stop him from building up the worry even further, she kissed him again, this time pouring all of her feelings into it until she felt him relax against her lips. "Let's not worry anymore for today. We're safe here." She looked up at him. "No one can touch me." She smiled. "Except you." She leaned in and kissed him, then took his hand in hers. "Take me upstairs."

CHAPTER EIGHTEEN

The worry he had for Bella was still playing in his mind as her lips moved over his. Then she reached for him and he forgot everything except her, here and now.

Lifting her into his arms, he carried her up the stairs as she tugged at his clothes, laughing when he had to stop in the middle of the stairs to yank off his pants.

"Here." She almost growled it out. "Please, I don't want to wait." She turned away from him, placing her hands on the banister on the small landing.

She glanced over her shoulder at him, and her tongue darted out and licked her bottom lip as her eyes ran slowly over him. He couldn't explain the powerful burst of lust that hit him while she looked at him with such desire.

Suddenly, he was yanking her pants off her hips. He sheathed himself and pushed her even further until she held onto the banister, her backside facing his desire as he plunged into her. She arched back as she cried out his name.

"Yes, please, Calvin." She jerked closer to him. His hands gripped her hips as she started moving, building his desire until he was almost blind with it.

Leaning forward, he gripped her breasts as she arched against his bare chest. His mouth nipped at her neck, her earlobes, until she cried out and he felt her tighten around him with her release.

Still, he wanted more. Needed more. Hoisting her up into his arms, he carried her lax body the rest of the way up to his bed. Laying her down gently, he waited until her eyes fluttered opened and focused on him.

"This matters," he said as he slowly slid into her.

"Yes," she agreed and wrapped her arms around him.

He bent down and kissed her, pouring everything he was into the kiss.

"You matter," he said as he felt himself slide.

He waited until he heard her breathing level and knew she was asleep before slipping out of bed to head downstairs and make sure he'd locked every door, every window. He quietly put the dishes in the dishwasher and started it. He noticed her phone sitting on the coffee table and took it upstairs. He plugged it in on her side of the bed, then crawled into the bed next to her and covered them both, pulling her into his arms.

First thing in the morning he was going to have a talk with Ben. He knew Bella had been hiding the extent of her dilemma from her brother. Ben had warned him not to hurt Bella, and he had no intention of doing so. Ever.

But that didn't mean the actions she'd taken in keeping her secrets hadn't hurt her brother and family.

When his alarm went off, he started to roll over, only to come up short when he realized the entire right side of his body was asleep.

Groaning, he peered out one eye and saw the messy mass of hair and smiled. "Morning," he said when she shifted, wrapping his arm tighter around her.

"Nooo," she sighed and tried to hold onto him. "Call in sick. The wedding was canceled."

He chuckled. "We still have guests. Actually, the groom is scheduled to leave this morning, and I wanted to make sure he has the proper send-off."

"I'll come with…" She started to roll away.

"No, don't. Your brother should be here by the time I leave. You're going to spend the day with them." He rolled her over until she was tucked underneath him. "And you're going to tell them everything."

She tensed, but then sighed and nodded. "Okay."

"Good." He leaned down and placed a soft kiss on her lips. "Now, I have less than half an hour to shower." He started moving against her and felt her warm up to him.

"A lot can happen in half an hour," she purred.

When Calvin let Ben in the back door, Bella was dressed in another pair of yoga pants along with one of his sweatshirts, eating toast and sipping coffee while she sat at his breakfast bar.

"Morning." Her brother walked in and set a box of donuts on the counter.

"My savior." She set the toast down and reached for the box.

"I thought you'd want something sugary this morning," Ben said, handing Calvin a to-go cup of coffee.

Calvin stopped himself from walking over and placing a kiss on Bella's lips before leaving. Instead, he reached in the box and took a donut for himself.

"See you later," he said as he started to walk away. Then Bella reached out, gripped his tie, and pulled him down until she brushed a soft kiss over his lips.

"Oh my god." Ben groaned. "Don't ever do that in front of me again."

"Shut up. You kiss Sarah all the time in front of me. It's practically the same thing." She smiled up at him. "Have a good day. Don't kill Fredrick."

He chuckled. "No promises," he said as he left. But before he walked out, he turned to her. "Show him the messages. All of them," he said with a frown.

Bella nodded, her smile slipping slightly.

"What messages?" Ben asked as Calvin shut the door behind him.

He knew Ben wouldn't let Bella be alone again while she was in town. She'd told him that she'd agreed to move back to Silver Cove after her commitments at the end of the month. Now, he just needed to convince her to move in with him instead of trying to get her own place.

Moving around that morning getting ready, just seeing her things in his closet and bathroom drawers made the place feel more like home than anything he'd ever done to the house.

Having her sit across from him on the kitchen bar while he'd downed his first cup of coffee and packed his lunch had brightened his morning. Falling asleep with her in his arms, making love to her into the late hours of the night, knowing that she would be there when he got off work. She'd embedded herself into his very core, and he didn't think he could breathe easily without knowing she was there.

Since the wedding event was canceled, most of the guests who hadn't left the evening before would be leaving today. Including, or so he'd been told by Brock, Fredrick Stafford. The guy had posted bail around midnight last night.

When Calvin stepped through the front door, he knew instantly it was going to be a long day. There was a line of guests trying to check out. Heather and Stacey were working the front counter and when they noticed him, they smiled.

"Here's the manager now," Stacey said with a sigh of relief.

An hour later, they'd checked everyone out and had assured them they would get refunds for the next two nights. He was about to head back to his office when Brock and Eric walked in.

Eric and Stacey were another stable couple Calvin enjoyed being around. This time, however, he could tell Eric was on official business.

"Got a moment?" Brock asked him.

"Sure." He nodded towards his office. The three of them started heading up the stairs. "Stacey, if you need me…"

The woman waved at him and then winked at her husband.

"What's this about?" he asked as he shut his office door.

"We got a call early this morning," Brock started. "Has Fredrick Stafford checked out yet?"

"No," Calvin answered with a frown. "I was waiting around downstairs so I could handle him personally."

"We found his rental car not far from the docks. The tires are slashed, and the inside is pretty messed up," Eric said.

"Car accident?" he asked.

"Nope, it's destroyed just the same though," Brock answered.

"Okay, so someone broke into it?"

"Could be. There was blood inside," Brock added. "Plenty of it. That's why we're looking for the man. The rental company wants to know what happened." He glanced towards the door. "Any chance we could take a look in his room?"

Calvin felt his stomach roll. "Sure." He stood up and the three of them headed back downstairs, where he had Stacey make him another key for the door and confirmed that the man hadn't checked out while they'd been upstairs.

He opened the door and waited for the two men to enter before stepping inside himself.

"Looks like his stuff is gone," Brock said.

Sure enough, the room was empty. It hadn't been cleaned yet, but he could see it was void of any personal effects.

"He hasn't checked out?" Brock turned to him.

Calvin frowned and shook his head. "After yesterday, I wouldn't be surprised if he snuck out in the middle of the night. What time did you say he made bail?"

"Just past midnight," Eric answered.

"Just for the record… You were where last night?" Brock asked.

Calvin sighed. "At home. Bella stayed with me. I texted Ben shortly after midnight to have him stay with Bella today." He pulled out his phone. "You can probably check the cell towers…"

"No need." Brock waved him off. "Just had to cross all the T's. You know. The guy probably banged up the rental car himself out of anger." He shook his head. "A man like that… loose cannon."

"He spat and cursed at me the entire time I booked him," Eric said with a chuckle.

"Well, it looks like the guy bailed." Brock stepped out of the room. Calvin spotted Sandra at the end of the hall and informed her she could clean that room next.

"Not checking out of a hotel isn't as bad as bailing on a rental car company after destroying their property." Brock sighed. "Consider yourself lucky he didn't trash the room too."

"Yeah," Calvin said following them down the stairs.

He watched as they headed out the front doors.

"Calvin?" Heather fell in step with him. "What's up?" She pointed towards the front door.

He stopped and looked at Heather. The woman had

worked as the resort's event coordinator longer than he'd been there. He knew that at one point she'd worked the front desk and still occasionally filled in when Stacey or Gavin was busy or needed a break. He liked Heather. She'd been one of the first friends he'd made when he had started working there.

"Looks like the groom slipped out sometime last night." He shrugged. "Put an extra charge on his card for not checking out properly then make sure the room is cleaned."

As he headed back up to his office, he thought of the sock to the jaw Ben had given him when he'd thought he was taking advantage of his little sister and wondered what kind of beating he'd take when he told him he was planning on getting his sister to move in with him. Shit.

The place was going to feel empty for a few days. The wedding party had pretty much rented out the entire resort, which meant every room was now sitting empty until Sunday.

Walking into his office, he pulled out his phone and shot Ben a quick message.

"Groom skipped out sometime last night."

Ben responded almost instantly. "Yeah? Good riddance from what Bella told me."

Calvin chuckled. "How's your sister?"

He had to wait for this response and was just about to set his phone down when it rang.

"That was too big of a response to type out," Ben said when Calvin answered the call.

"Okay," he waited.

"She's good. She and Sarah are out shopping."

"Again? She dragged me all over town yesterday," he joked.

"Food shopping. They're planning a dinner tonight. Which you are required to attend," Ben said.

"I'll be there. Your place?" he asked.

"You know it. JT and family are coming as well. My sister wanted to see the twins."

"Sounds good." He waited for a moment then changed the subject. "Did she show you the messages?"

The phone went quiet for a moment. "Yeah. I called the cops in charge in LA."

"And?" he asked. He'd thought of doing that himself but figured Ben would get to the bottom of it before he had a chance to.

"They seem competent. They don't think it's someone in LA. Which was a surprise to me."

"Why don't they?" He frowned.

"Well, a few reasons. The burner SIM cards the messages came from were sold in a store in Colorado."

"So, they have the guy's information then?"

"No, they were cash sales." Ben sighed. "But they believe he traveled to LA to break into her apartment."

"Wait." Calvin stood up. "Her place has been broken into before?" He felt his temper grow.

"I know what you're thinking, but she wasn't there and that time nothing was disturbed. He left a threatening message, which is when the police got involved." Calvin took a couple of deep breaths as he sat down again. "It was the week before she came out here. She followed the police's advice and came out here. They've had a look-alike staying at her place. Well, they did, until the break-in yesterday."

"They were trying to catch the guy that way?"

"Yeah. They think the picture of you and Bella on the sailboat here blew that plan out of the water." Ben took a deep breath. "We still don't know how they found out she was here in town and not LA."

"I asked all the staff. Everyone claims they didn't spill.

Because of our clients, when we hire them, they sign an NDA."

"That never stopped someone who wants a little extra cash. I talked Brock into having a chat with the reporters he chased out of town," Ben said.

"Are we sure they're gone?" he asked, thinking about the stolen items and the ladder. Could it have been one of the paparazzi trying to use it to get a picture of Bella? Then why use the shears to cut up her things? That screamed it was personal not professional.

He thought of where he'd found the ladder and if they could have had a view into her rooms from there. He didn't think so, but as soon as he could, he was going to walk out there and make sure.

"According to Brock, he warned the bunch of them that if they were spotted in Silver Cove again, they'd be arrested. Then he warned the vendor who rented them the boats. When the guy heard that the group had harassed Bella, he'd been pissed and swore he'd watch out for them."

"Good." Calvin relaxed slightly. He knew that everyone in Silver Cove looked out for their own and since Bella had come to town when she was younger, she'd been one of their own.

It had taken a little over a year for Calvin to be accepted into the fold. The moment he'd purchased his sailboat, the *Dame*, he was officially deemed a local.

"I'll keep you posted. They're looking into what Brock sent them on the break-in there. How's the room?"

Ben had a list of items that needed to be replaced in the suite. "About three thousand dollars' worth of damage," he calculated. "It could have been worse. The jilted groom could have destroyed his room too."

"That's what insurance is for." Ben sighed. "It's Bella I'm more worried about. She's jumping at shadows."

"Yeah," he agreed, remembering last night's conversation with her. "Keep me in the loop, will you?"

Ben chuckled. "I may not have liked it at first, but you are family now." He sighed. "Sorry about the loose jaw."

Calvin smiled. "It's not loose. Remember? You punch like a—" Ben hung up the phone, causing Calvin to laugh.

CHAPTER NINETEEN

It was nice, sitting around a large table with people you loved. The room was filled with laughter and the chatter of kids.

Her nieces had glued themselves to Calvin the moment he'd walked in her brother's front door. That was until Sarah grabbed them up and placed them both in their highchairs to eat.

She'd enjoyed cooking the salmon dinner with Sarah. It reminded her of all the times she'd cooked with Sarah when she'd lived there.

Emma was nothing like she'd imagined she would be. She'd met plenty of actresses in Hollywood while she'd been out there. Even though Emma was an up-and-coming name and face on the screen, she fit in Silver Cove easily. She was more down to earth than any other actress Bella had met.

JT and Emma were perfect new parents to the little boy and girl. It was so funny how after an hour with them, she couldn't imagine them not having the kids or being together.

After dinner, they all moved into the living room where the kids played as the adults sat around and talked.

She knew she needed to tell her brother that she was planning on moving back to Silver Cove. She hadn't even talked to her agent yet to see when in her schedule she had time to move.

Not that she had to ask permission to move, but Maggie did fill her schedule.

One thing was clear to her—she felt safer surrounded by family and friends, even though she was pretty sure Michael had sent some goons out here to intimidate her.

Maggie had assured her that since she'd been in Maine, Michael hadn't left California once.

It would have been a lot easier if Michael had come himself. Then they could have pinned the break-in on him and officially charged him. After all, Michael was even more famous than she was. The few times she'd been with him, he hadn't even been able to walk in a door without someone calling out his name or asking for a signature.

"You're quiet." Ben broke into her thoughts.

She glanced around and realized that Sarah and Lilly had disappeared with the kids.

"Sorry." She shook her head. "Deep in thought." She shrugged.

"About the break-in?" her brother asked.

She sighed and glanced at Calvin, who nodded his encouragement to her.

"Yes," she started as Calvin took her hand in his. Somehow the light contact gave her more strength and courage to tell her brother her plans. But before she could open her mouth to speak again, Ben jumped in.

"We think you should move back home," her brother said.

She swallowed before talking. "I was planning on it."

"I don't care what… wait…" Her brother's eyebrows drew up. "You were?"

"Yes." She smiled. "I'd talked it over with Calvin and…"

"She's going to be moving in with me," Calvin said, his eyes searching hers as if waiting for her to deny it. Instead, she nodded.

Ben chuckled. "You don't know what you're in for there." Ben reached over and slapped Calvin on the shoulder. "She never does dishes."

Bella opened her mouth to argue but then laughed. "It's true." She shrugged.

Calvin squeezed her hand. "It won't be a requirement."

"Then it's settled." Ben clapped his hands and leaned back. "When do we go get your stuff?"

A few hours later, she was lying in Calvin's arms in his bed as he stroked a hand down her bare back.

"Somehow I didn't think that telling my brother would be that easy." She felt her entire body relax.

She felt Calvin's chest rumble with his laughter. "Why not?"

She shrugged, but since she was half-asleep, she barely moved. "I suppose I thought that he'd think I was giving up on my career."

He stilled and then glanced down at her. "Do you think you're giving up?"

She thought about it for a moment before answering. "No matter what, I am not going to let Michael ruin my singing career. I can live anywhere and record. I don't have to be in LA."

He relaxed and she heard him sigh. "He won't ruin you," he said softly. "You're too strong to let anyone take you down like that."

"But?" She leaned up and looked down at him when she heard the reservation in his tone.

He reached up and brushed a strand of her hair away from her face.

"It doesn't mean that I don't worry about you. If you had been staying in your rooms that night…"

She closed her eyes at the dark thoughts she'd had about what could have happened if she hadn't been staying with Calvin that night.

"I know." She shivered and his hands tightened around her. "But I can't keep living in fear." She raised her chin slightly. "I've got a few commitments for my album release next week. Maggie has scheduled an interview in two days at the resort."

"Yeah, I saw it on the schedule today." He shifted, bringing her back down to his chest. "Are you sure you're up for it?"

"Will you be there?" she asked, closing her eyes.

"Yes," he responded quickly.

"Then, I'm ready." She yawned and snuggled further into his chest.

Shortly before Calvin left for work the following day, Sarah and the girls showed up with more baked goods.

"If this keeps up, I'll have to roll back into LA," she joked as she held Luna in her lap. The girls had warmed up to her after last night. Seeing her with Calvin had solidified to them that she was okay to be with.

That and she'd helped cart them around the stores while Sarah had done the shopping.

"What's all this?" Calvin said as he came over to her and kissed the top of Luna's head and then repeated the motion with her head.

"Breakfasss." Aurora giggled as he reached over and tickled her and then gave her sloppy kisses. "Cal, spin?" Aurora reached for him with fingers covered in frosting.

"No," Sarah jumped in. "Calvin is all dressed up and ready for work." She quickly wiped her daughter's fingers before she could damage anything else within a five-foot radius.

"Sorry, bug, how about later?" Calvin frowned down at

Aurora.

The little girl frowned but then was easily distracted when Sarah handed her a cup of milk.

"Here." Sarah shifted a box of donuts towards Calvin. "Have some."

He chuckled and patted his stomach. "I think I'll pass. If I keep eating sweets, I'll have to hit the gym every night this week. I'll grab something at work." He leaned in and kissed her. "Have a good day," he told her. "I'll see you for dinner."

"Which will be at Lilly and Adam's place," Sarah piped in. "I'll be dropping Bella off there just before you get off work. We've got reading at the library tonight." She sighed. "It's the one night I can sit back and not worry about the girls breaking anything."

He chuckled and then leaned in and kissed Sarah on the cheek. "You're a wonderful mother."

Sarah brightened. "I know." She laughed and pushed him towards the door. "Go. You don't want to be late. Your boss will…" Calvin's eyebrows shot up and Sarah laughed. "He'll probably not do anything, but you don't want to miss the ferry."

"True." He laughed as he left.

"So." Sarah turned back to her. "Are you going to tell me everything?" Her sister-in-law leaned on the counter as she handed Luna her sippy cup of milk and took away the new donut the girl had wiggled out of the box.

Bella chuckled. "Prying ears…" She nodded to the girls.

"They don't know what the heck we're talking about most of the time. At least not yet. Except when we happen to use choice words." She frowned. "Those, they repeat at the worst times." She held in a chuckle and rolled her eyes. "Luna said…"—she glanced over at her youngest and whispered— "the S word last week at a playdate."

Bella laughed. "Is that why you were mad at Ben when I

arrived?"

"No." Sarah sighed. "That one she heard from me."

Bella laughed harder.

After cleaning up the breakfast mess, Bella headed upstairs to shower and change for the day. When she came back down, the girls were asleep in front of the television, which had cartoons playing and the volume low. Even Sarah's eyes were closed as she held Luna against her chest.

Not wanting to disturb them, she sat down and pulled out her phone to type a message to Maggie. She must have retyped the message more than a dozen times before hitting send.

Thankfully, she'd muted her phone because a few moments later, it rang.

Stepping out on the back deck, she answered the call.

"What do you mean you're moving back to Maine?" Maggie's voice was raised slightly as if she was breathless.

"Just what I said. I'll be moving back home. I can still fulfill my commitment for the second album and fly out for all the promotional—"

"Is this because of Michael?" Maggie broke in and asked.

"No," she answered, knowing it was the truth. Maybe part of the reason for the move was, but her main reason was Calvin.

She leaned against the deck and looked out over the water as she talked on the phone. The view was amazing here. If she leaned over a little, she could probably see the resort.

"You're not listening to me." Maggie's tone snapped her back.

"Sorry." She sighed. "Mags, I've met the man of my dreams." She smiled. "I'm moving in with him. Here."

Maggie was quiet. "That's all so… sudden. What do you know about this man?"

Bella laughed. "I've known him most of my life." She shifted the phone to her other ear. "He's my brother Ben's best friend."

"The hunk in the boat?" Maggie asked, her tone turning softer.

"Yes." She smiled. "Calvin Winters. He runs my brother and sister-in-law's resort up here."

"East Haven? Where they're doing your interview tomorrow?" Maggie asked, her tone turning a little worried.

"Yes," she answered with a frown. "Why?"

"It's… nothing," Maggie finished.

"What?" Bella straightened.

"It's just… after that picture of the two of you went crazy, I did a little research into your man… You know, just in case he had something dark in his past that the press could use against you…"

"And?" Bella frowned. She'd known Calvin for so long, she doubted there was anything in his past that she or Ben didn't know about. If Calvin had done anything bad, her brother wouldn't have remained best friends with him.

"Well, it's just…"

"Spit it out," she said, frowning.

"It seems that he killed his younger sister," Maggie said hesitantly.

"What?" Bella almost screamed it as she shook her head. "No." She laughed, feeling relieved. "You've obviously got the wrong—"

"Calvin Winters, parents are…" Bella heard Maggie shifting some papers around. "Tammy and Adam Winters. He has a younger brother named James. He attended Le Rosey Private Boarding School in Switzerland with your brother Ben. The report from back then says that he was a few weeks shy of his thirteenth birthday and his sister was five years old at the time. Her name was Kelly Winters…"

Bella's vision grayed as a loud buzzing filled her ears. She moved over to sit down on a chair before she passed out or fell over the edge of the deck.

"Bella?" Maggie's voice finally broke through.

"I...I'll call you back later." She hung up and sat there staring into space until Sarah stepped out with a crying Luna on her hip. "Sorry, we must have checked out." She giggled but stopped when she noticed Bella's look. "Is everything okay?" Sarah glanced around as if looking for whatever had caused Bella to be upset.

"Yes, I guess I was just deep in thought," Bella answered automatically. Whatever happened now, she figured there was no way Ben or Sarah knew what Calvin had done. So, no matter what, she was going to make sure they didn't find out about Calvin's dark past. "Ready to head out?" She stood up, dusting off her jeans.

The rest of the day, the knowledge of what Calvin had done loomed over her, darkening her mood. Thankfully, Sarah was so busy with the girls that she didn't have time to notice. When Sarah dropped her off at Lilly and Adam's place just a few blocks down from their home, she had worried so much that she had a headache.

"You look tired," Lilly said as she stepped into their house.

"I guess I didn't realize how much two young kids can wear you out," she joked.

"Why don't you head up to our guest room and lie down for a while. Adam's in control in the kitchen, and I've got to get the kids ready before Calvin gets here." She motioned towards the stairs. "Third door on the right." She smiled. "If you need it, there is aspirin in the bathroom medicine cabinet."

"Thanks." Bella moved towards the stairs, but stopped and hugged Lilly. "Thanks," she said again.

CHAPTER TWENTY

When Calvin stepped into Lilly and Adam's home shortly after he'd gotten off work, he instantly questioned how quiet it was.

"The kids are already down for the night." Lilly smiled at him as she waved a baby monitor. "We fed them early so we could enjoy a quiet evening."

"I was looking forward to tickling them," he joked.

"Next time." Lilly hugged him. "Adam says dinner's almost ready."

As he moved further into their home, he glanced around. He'd been in their place more times than he could count. "Did Sarah drop Bella off yet?"

Lilly glanced towards the stairs. "She went up and laid down." She touched his arm. "She looked tired when she got here. She made some excuse about how the kids had worn her out, but there was sadness behind her eyes. I think something else happened."

He stiffened and glanced towards the stairs.

"Third door on the right." Lilly nudged him towards the stairs.

When he opened the door, the room was dark, but he could just make out a bump in the middle of the bed. Moving over, he sat on the edge of the bed and reached for her.

She rolled over and for a moment he thought she would go willingly into his arms, but then she stiffened and sat up.

"Sorry." She glanced around then ran her hands over her face. "I must have fallen asleep."

"How are you feeling?" he asked, wishing for a little more light so that he could see her face clearly.

"Better," she said as she moved to get off the bed. He helped her stand and felt her stiffen in his arms.

He wanted to ask her what the problem was, but she made her way towards the bedroom door. "I'd better go see if I can help Lilly."

He stood in the bedroom for a moment, wondering what he'd done to cause her cold shoulder, then followed her downstairs.

Dinner was nice, if he didn't focus on the fact that Bella pretty much ignored him the entire meal. She talked quietly with Lilly while Adam and he joked about sports, fishing, and work.

Still, he figured she was tired or fighting off a headache.

When dinner was over, instead of letting the couple talk them into staying a little longer, he faked being tired and excused them. Normally, he would have walked to their place, but since he'd read that it was supposed to rain that evening, he'd pulled out his Jeep and had driven the few blocks. Now, he was thankful he had. As he helped Bella up into the Jeep, he realized just how tired she was.

"Tired?" he asked as he got behind the wheel.

"Yes," she said softly as she looked out the window as he drove. Just as he pulled into his driveway, she turned to him and added. "I didn't know you had a Jeep."

"There's probably lots about me you haven't discovered

yet," he joked as he parked in his garage and shut off the engine.

The last thing he expected was tears to flood her eyes. "Hey, what's all this about?" He reached for her, but she jerked back.

"I didn't know you had a sister either." It was like a punch to the gut. His hand dropped away, and he felt his pulse jump. "One that you supposedly killed." She reached for the Jeep door.

He closed his eyes. No matter how long it had been, no matter how many times he'd talked himself out of it, tears still stung his eyes as his breath caught in his chest.

"Calvin?" Bella's voice broke through the haze of the nightmare that always came with the memories. When she touched his arm, this time it was him that jerked away.

"I told you, there's lots about me you wouldn't like," he spat out, knowing it was for the best. What had he been thinking? He didn't deserve Happy Ever Afters. Bella was too… perfect. Too good for him.

He knew that he'd screw it up. He always did. That's what his parents had believed. That's why they'd sent him away to boarding school. Because he was a fuckup.

"Calvin, talk to me." She shook his shoulder. Instead of responding, he climbed out of the Jeep and marched into the house with her on his heels.

"What?" He turned around, angry now. Not at her, but at himself for letting down his guard. For believing he deserved being with her. To think that he was good enough that she would move in here with him and he could just ignore the fact that he was the reason his sister wasn't alive.

"What happened?" she asked, moving over to him.

"Don't you know?" He walked over to the fridge and pulled out a beer. After a sip of it, he frowned and set it down, reaching for a soda instead. He paced the floor as she watched him.

"No, I guess I don't," she answered with a frown. "Maggie—"

He turned on her. "Your agent?"

She nodded slowly as she bit her bottom lip. He could see the concern in her eyes, which had replaced the weariness from earlier. "She… well, after the picture was leaked of us on the sailboat… your sailboat," she corrected with a tilt of her head, "she didn't want the press to be able to find any dirt on you…"

"So, she found it herself?" He set the can of soda down and walked over to the back doors and slid them open. He stepped out into the cool night air, just as the first raindrops hit. Thankfully, there was enough overhang on the roof that he would stay dry as he gulped in the fresh air.

"She wouldn't have had to say anything to me if you'd told me yourself," she said from behind him.

He turned and looked at her. The light from the kitchen behind her cast a glow around her as if reaffirming that she was untouchable. He turned away from her and leaned against the railing to look out over the stormy water below them.

"I told you from the beginning this wouldn't work." He closed his eyes on the pain of losing her. He'd lost so much early on in his life; he should have been used to it by now.

Her arms wrapped around his waist as she turned him towards her. "I'm sorry. I shouldn't have jumped to conclusions."

He shook his head. "Whatever you're thinking, it's probably not as bad as what really happened."

Her eyes narrowed, then she shook her head. "You could never harm someone on purpose. You don't have it in you."

"How do you know?" he asked as her arms tightened around him.

"Because…" She reached up and touched his chest. "It's in here." She smiled up at him. "I was blindsided and I'm sorry I didn't defend you."

"There's nothing to defend." He wanted to push her away, but she was holding onto him too tight and, besides, it felt too good.

She asked. "Does my brother know?"

He sighed. "Yes, it happened months before we met. He was the only one who wanted to be friends with me at school when all the other kids had labeled me a baby killer." He shook his head on the painful memories. "She wasn't a baby. Kelly was…" His throat closed as love and loss battled in his mind. "She was smart. She was so smart, and she was running around, everywhere. So full of energy."

He hadn't realized tears were sliding down his cheek until Bella reached up and wiped them away with her fingers.

"You loved her," she said with a slight smile.

"Of course, I did. We all did. She was the best of the family." He sighed. "She was the only thing that held us together. After her death… things changed. Everyone changed."

"You were shipped across the world," she supplied.

"I deserved it." He frowned down at her.

"Why?" She shook her head.

He glanced back out at the darkness beyond his deck and thought about the day that had changed his life.

"I was twelve years old. I was stoked about my upcoming thirteenth birthday party. I'd been told I could invite girls." He looked down at her. "I was really excited."

She nodded with a slight smile. "I get that."

"Well, the parents had asked me to watch Kelly for a few hours while they ran to the country club for lunch. They often did that. Even though they loved Kelly, they liked socializing without a five-year-old asking them a million questions. I was on the phone with my friends, trying to come up with a list of girls we were going to ask to the party. Kelly wanted to play outside on the new swing set the folks had gotten her for her birthday. You know, one of those tree fort things with swings, slides, and a little fort on top."

She nodded. "I know the kind."

He took a deep breath. "I just ran inside for some paper and a pen. To make the list of everyone my friends and I wanted to invite. When I came back out… well, I thought she was still up in the fort part. It wasn't until I got off the phone and started looking around that I realized she wasn't in the yard."

"What happened?" she asked with a frown.

Instead of answering, he took her hands and walked them over to sit on a swing closer to the house so the rain, which had grown heavier, wouldn't splash them. After they sat down, he continued.

"I searched everywhere. I got my little brother, who had been inside playing video games, to help me search the house, the yard, and even run to a few neighbors to make sure she hadn't wandered over there to play. When we didn't find her, we called the folks. At first, they were upset that I'd interrupted their lunch date." He laughed, remembering how annoyed his father had been. "Then I told them Kelly was missing." He closed his eyes and shivered at the memory. "The police came and started searching. I must have told my story more than a dozen times. At one point, they even hauled me into the police station, separated me from my folks, and grilled me." He took a deep breath. "I had never been more afraid in my life."

He glanced over at Bella and could tell she was hanging on his every word.

"It took less than a week to find her body across town in a

dumpster. Someone had…" His voice broke and he shut his eyes again as another fresh tear slipped down his cheek. "They'd abused her and left her like a piece of trash. At first, everyone was blaming me for not watching her. Some even believed I had something to do with her disappearance."

"Calvin." She wrapped her arms around him and held on. "I'm so sorry."

Just feeling her next to him eased the pain of the memories. "I should have…"

She surprised him by pulling away and taking his face in her hands.

"They left a preteen boy in charge of a five-year-old to go socialize," she said, her eyes burning into his. "Predators will always find a way. You couldn't have known. Did they catch the person?"

He nodded. "Thanks to DNA. It was a worker my parents used a few times around the house. They had hired him to paint Kelly's bedroom for her birthday, and he even installed her new swing set. The one he took her from that day."

"I'm so sorry," she said again. Then she tilted her head. "They shipped you off to boarding school after that?"

He nodded and looked down at their joined hands. Suddenly, she stood up and started pacing in front of him. Then after a moment of that, she turned on him.

"They shipped you off after someone they let into their home stalked, kidnapped, then murdered your little sister." Her voice rose and he watched her cross her arms over her chest. "They blamed you?"

He swallowed and nodded slightly. "It was my…"

"Don't you dare say it was your fault." She moved closer to you. "You are as much a victim as your sister was. You were twelve," she said, dragging out the word as if it would explain everything. "You didn't kidnap her. You didn't let your sister go willingly with the man. You didn't murder her.

You were just a kid. A boy who had just lost his little sister and blamed himself for not watching her. Then they shipped you off like… like…" She threw up her hands. "Like you were a murderer yourself."

He sighed. "I was, in some way."

"Calvin Winters, you are no more responsible for your sister's death than I am. Your parents shipped you away because they couldn't stand their own guilt. They threw the blame solely on your shoulders and then pushed you away to cover it up."

He stood up and wrapped his arms around her, then placed a kiss on the top of her head. "You're amazing." He took in the feeling of her, the scent of her and knew that it would probably be the last time he'd hold her. After everything he'd just confessed, he knew that with her life, they couldn't be together. Part of his heart broke, just like it had the day they'd found Kelly's body.

CHAPTER TWENTY-ONE

She could tell that Calvin was struggling with what he'd told her. He didn't see it the same way she did. The more she thought about it, the angrier she was at his parents. How could parents let a kid believe he was at fault for something so far out of his control?

Did they still treat him as if his sister's death was on him?

The way he was holding her as the rain fell a few feet away from them told her that he believed she was going to leave him. That thought broke her heart.

He was so damaged by his selfish parents that all of her problems with her own self-absorbed parents seemed minuscule.

"Calvin." She pulled back and leaned up on her toes to place a soft kiss on his lips. "Know that I don't blame you at all. In fact, if I ever get a chance, I'm going to have a serious talk with your parents about their treatment of you." She touched his face, enjoying the softness of the light beard he'd grown out. "I'd be happy to set them straight. We all have things in our past. Albeit yours is pretty… heavy. But as I said, I don't believe your sister's death was on you at all. I'm sorry your parents made you believe you'd done something wrong."

He sighed and nodded. "As a rational adult—which I would like to think that I have become—I agree with you. But it's taken me years to finally come to terms with that." He shook his head again. "I found it easier to never talk to my parents about it since we don't see eye to eye on the topic." He shrugged and glanced over as lightning filled the sky. "Come on, we'd better go inside."

She took his hand and tugged him inside. He locked the door and shut the blinds behind them. Before he could move away, she wrapped her arms around him again.

"You aren't going to use this as an excuse to not allow me to move in here with you, are you?" She smiled up at him.

He looked a little shocked, then asked. "Are you sure you want to? I didn't mean to pressure you into moving in with me. I had planned on asking you… before blurting it out to Ben."

She laughed. "Try and stop me from moving in here." She kissed him again and could feel that the dark mood was gone even though outside the storm grew stronger.

He shook his head as his hands started moving over her hips. She'd pressed her body close to him and wanted more than anything for him to carry her upstairs and make love with her all night.

She'd had enough rollercoaster emotions for one day. Now she wanted to fall asleep in the arms of the man she loved.

Realizing that she hadn't actually said those words to him yet, she smiled.

Taking his hand, she pulled him towards the stairs. "You know that sexy little pink lace thing I bought the other day?"

His eyebrows shot up quickly and a smile lit his face. "The one with the straps?"

She chuckled. "I'm wearing it…" She dropped his hand and started up the stairs. "Under this outfit. If you hurry, you might just get to help me peel it off…" He picked her up in his arms and carried her the rest of the way upstairs as she laughed.

After he shut them in his bedroom, he slid her down as he kissed her. She felt her entire body melt as his hands pulled her clothes aside. Her fingers shook as she unbuttoned his shirt. She slipped the tie off him, then pulled the shirt wide so she could appreciate his tanned, toned chest.

"Mm." She smiled before leaning in and running kisses over the play of muscles that covered him. "I could get used to seeing this every day." She ran her fingertips over him, letting her short nails scrape lightly over his skin. She noticed small little bumps raise all over him and smiled. "You like that?" she asked.

"God," he said in a burst, "you make me so hard." He took her hand and moved it to his crotch. She rubbed him as her smile grew. He began to peel off her blouse. When he exposed the pink silk, he groaned and bent his head to run his mouth over the material.

She arched back and watched as he sucked the material over her nipple, making it harden for him. Her fingers slid into his hair, holding him as he ran his tongue over her skin and the edge of the silk.

"You taste like spring," he said as he reached for her jeans. When they pooled at her feet, she stepped out of the jeans, and he nudged her closer to the bed.

"Bella," he said when his mouth returned to hers, "I can't imagine what I've done in life to deserve you."

"Nothing." She smiled at him. "We're just lucky to find each other I guess," she said as he ran his eyes slowly over her. She was standing before him in nothing but pink silk, feeling like the most beautiful woman on earth.

She reached for the clasp of his slacks, keeping her eyes on his as she pushed them off his narrow hips. As she ran her hands over his muscular thighs and tight stomach, she thought she heard him sigh, "Tell me."

"Calvin." She looked up into his eyes again. "I wanted you to know, before... I love you." She leaned up and kissed him again. She thought she felt him stiffen, but then he was pushing her down onto the bed and covering her body with his.

She'd dreamed of how it would be when she finally told a man those words. Feeling the speed and heat of desire consume her hadn't been part of those plans. She couldn't have ever dreamed of how wonderful it would feel to be with someone she loved.

When the last layers of material were gone between them, he arched over her, his hands running up her body until he clasped hers above her head.

"I didn't believe I deserved this, you." He kissed her again as she wrapped her legs around him, trying to pull him closer. "Bella, I've loved you for a while now. I tried to deny it." He pulled back and looked down into her eyes, then shook his head and smiled. "I was a fool to think I could give you up. It's the sweetest surrender I've had, giving you my heart." He kissed her again and then, as he slid into her, he whispered next to her ear, "I love you."

She must have fallen asleep after he rolled to her side, tucking their bodies close together and pulling the comforter over them.

His steady heartbeat soothed her, relaxed her, even though the storm still raged outside the large glass doors and windows in his bedroom.

When a large crash of thunder woke her, her heart jumped in her chest as the sound dissipated through the dark house. She lay there, Calvin's arms wrapped tightly around her, as she tried to settle her heart back down.

Then another flash of lightning lit the room and she noticed the dark shadow of a man standing by the glass doors that led out to the deck. Her entire body froze with fear as the scream caught in her throat.

Her body began to shake as the thunder from the lightning finally sounded a few seconds later. Her eyes strained as she tried to see if the figure had moved.

It seemed to take forever for her body to finally respond to her commands. Her mind played out a million scenarios of what she should do.

Deciding finally to reach for the lamp and wake Calvin at the same time, she screamed as she flipped on the bedside lamp.

Calvin jumped from the bed as the light flooded the room, showcasing that they were alone.

"What?" Calvin glanced around, blinking a few times.

"Someone was in the room." She pointed to the spot where the glass doors stood wide open.

Calvin reached under the bed and came up with a metal baseball bat. "Call the police," he said as he rushed into the rain in nothing but a pair of boxer briefs.

She blinked and stared at the wet footprints just inside the patio doors. Her hand shook as she reached for her cell phone and called the police.

Her eyes were glued to the doors as she waited for Calvin to return. The police had assured her that a patrol car was on its way just as Calvin stepped back inside.

"Wait," she called out, stopping him from messing up the wet footprints. She pointed to them and Calvin easily moved around them, leaving them undisturbed. "Did you find anyone?" she asked.

"No, they took off too quickly. I saw taillights." He pulled on his jeans and shoes, then a jacket. "I'm going to wait for the police." He nodded to her. "Better get dressed." He walked over and wrapped his arms around her. "Are you okay?" he asked after she stood there for a moment.

"Y-yes." She took a deep breath. "He was just standing there. Watching us." She shivered.

Calvin's arms tightened around her. "He broke the door lock." He motioned towards the sliding door. "First thing tomorrow, I'm installing cameras and a security system." She nodded as they heard the siren. "Get dressed. I'll go down and meet them."

She watched him go, then slipped on her clothes quickly, grabbing one of his sweaters and pulling it over her head instead of trying to find something warm of her own to wear. Walking by, she snapped a picture of the watery footprints and the lock on the door that had been jimmied open.

When she stepped out of the bedroom, Calvin was talking with Brock. Both men turned up to watch her make her way down the stairs.

"Bella." Brock nodded. "How are you doing?"

"I've settled down. I think my heart rate is finally leveled." She chuckled nervously.

"Well, if it's okay, I'll head up and take pictures and see if I can spot anything else up there." Brock nodded towards the stairs.

"I'm done sleeping up there for tonight," she admitted. "Coffee?" she asked, walking into the kitchen.

"I wouldn't say no to a cup." Brock smiled. "I'll be back." Calvin led him up the stairs.

By the time they came back down, Ben was standing in the kitchen, sipping a cup of coffee with her.

"You called Ben?" she'd asked Calvin when Ben had arrived.

"Duh." He walked over and wrapped his arms around her.

"I'm not stupid. If he found out about this from Brock…" He hissed. "I'd be in it deep."

She smiled. "Thank you." She kissed him.

The moment her brother had rushed into the house, she'd felt better. He'd wrapped his arms around her, and she'd cried for a moment, then she'd fixed them each a cup of coffee and found a bag of cookies to munch on while they waited.

"What did you find?" Ben asked Brock.

"Broken lock on the sliding door, wet boot prints, size eleven, and muddy tire marks that I snapped a picture of but will be gone by the time the crew gets here to take a mold." He sighed. "Hopefully, we can ID them by the picture." He waved his phone. Brock turned to her. "Any idea on how tall the guy was?"

She shook her head as she handed Brock a mug of coffee then handed one to Calvin. "No, it was just a flash. I mean, I only saw him when the lightning filled the room. I must have woken up to the sound of him sliding open the door. I thought…" She shook her head, trying to remember anything. Why had she woken up? But she'd been so deep in sleep, everything was fuzzy in her mind.

"Since we know where he stood, can you tell me if he filled the doorway?" He walked over to the sliding doors like the ones in the bedroom and stood approximately where the footprints had been then held up his hand to the top of his head. "Was he as tall as me?"

She tilted her head, then set her mug down and moved over to lay on the sofa. Turning her head, she looked at Brock and shrugged. "That looks about right."

"Calvin, come here." He waved his hand and Calvin took his place. "Or does this look closer?"

Bella shook her head. "No, Calvin is too tall. I can't see the top of the door with him."

"Okay." Brock waved Ben over.

Ben stood where they had, and Bella nodded. Yeah, it's between you and Ben." She sat up.

"Okay." Brock wrote something down in the notepad. "Between five-nine and..." He glanced over at Ben. "You're still six?" he asked.

"Yes," Ben said with a slight frown.

"Okay, between five-nine and six-foot." He nodded to Ben. "Did you happen to notice anything else about the man?"

She thought about it. "He was wearing all black." She shrugged. "I didn't see his face clearly." She thought about it. "He had very pale skin, or he was wearing a white face mask." She shook her head. "Sorry." She closed her eyes. "I was half-asleep."

"It's okay. At least we have some things to go on," Brock said. "Calvin says he's going to be installing a security system tomorrow."

"I'll be here to help," Ben jumped in.

Brock turned to Bella. "I'll keep you posted if we find anything on those tire tracks."

"I'm sorry I can't remember more," she said.

"If you do, you know where to find us." He took a large sip of the coffee and set the mug down. "Thanks for the cup."

Calvin walked Brock out as Ben wrapped his arms around her again. "Want to come to our place for the rest of the night?"

She thought about going back upstairs with the busted lock and shivered. Then she thought of putting her nieces or Sarah in danger and shook her head.

"No," she answered. "I'm wide awake now. I think I'll make some breakfast and try and get some work done."

Ben groaned. "I thought you'd say that. I guess I'll be heading to the hardware store when they open and getting everything you guys need." He glanced over at the stove then laughed. "Don't cook. I'll run and get us something from the bakery. They open..."—he glanced down at his watch and sighed— "ten minutes from now."

She smiled. "Thanks."

"Why can't psychopaths do this shit in the middle of the day instead of the middle of the night?" Ben complained.

"It's almost six," Calvin pointed out as he walked back inside and removed his raincoat. "I'll get started on fixing the door."

"I'll head in and get us some breakfast. The hardware store won't open until eight." He groaned. "Gotta call Sarah and let her know what's up." He turned back to Calvin. "Call and see if someone can cover your shift." He started to walk out then stopped. "For the next week. I don't want you leaving my sister's side until we catch this madman."

"Yes, boss." Calvin saluted him with a smile.

"Shove it," Ben groaned as he left.

"He needs sugar to wake up," she explained. "More coffee?" she asked, pouring herself another cup.

Calvin's arms wrapped around her, and she set her mug down and enjoyed the feeling of him holding her. "I'm sorry," he said into her hair.

"For?" she asked turning in his arms and wrapping her arms around him.

"I should have..."

"There you go, blaming yourself again for things that are out of your control." She reached up and kissed him.

He sighed and nodded, resting his forehead against hers. "You're right." His eyes met hers. "I'm going to make this place a fortress for you. I don't ever want you to feel unsafe here again."

She nodded. "I'd like that." She smiled. "Now, can I help you fix the door?"

When her brother and Rowan walked in half an hour later with two boxes of donuts, they had finished fixing the lock on the door and had added a metal bar that would slide between the two doors for extra security. He even added the bars to the three other sliding doors in the house. Since the windows all rolled vertically and had little childhood locks on them already, no one could easily break those open without shattering the windows.

"I brought help." Ben pointed to Rowan. "I ran into him at the Donut Hut and told him what happened. He volunteered to help install the new system."

"I installed one a few years back." Rowan shrugged. "It's not that hard."

"I helped," Ben added as he took a large chocolate-covered donut and bit into it.

"Yes." Rowan slapped him on the shoulder. "You held the ladder for me if my memory serves me," he joked.

"Shove it," Ben said through a full mouth, but it ended up sounding more like "Suvt."

"Now, boys," Bella said with a laugh as she took a sprin-kled donut for herself. "Let's all play nicely."

CHAPTER TWENTY-TWO

*W*orking with his friends on installing the top-of-the-line security system around his house was like old times. It reminded him of the year they'd all worked together getting the house fixed up.

"Remind me why we don't do this sort of thing more often?" Ben joked as he held the ladder for Rowan as he drilled a hole for the camera wire.

"Because you stand around drinking beer while we do all the work," Calvin joked.

The rain had let up shortly after Brock had left. The early morning mist had been burned off by the sun and now there was a bead of sweat rolling down his back as he felt his skin burn in the sun.

Sarah had shown up an hour after Ben had come back from the hardware store. She'd dropped the kids off at her mother's and was keeping Bella entertained by listening to her play on her old guitar, which she'd brought over from their house.

He had to admit, listening to her play and sing was a pure joy. He even caught Rowan singing along to one of her songs.

"You know this?" he asked him with a nudge.

"Sure do. It's Kayla and CJ's favorite." He smiled then frowned. "Don't you?"

Calvin felt like a fool for being with Bella but not knowing the words to any of her songs, so he shrugged and busied himself.

He promised himself that the first chance he got alone, he'd listen to her songs and memorize the words. After all, she'd written them all herself. The least he could do is hear them at least once.

At one point, the ladies ran to the grocery store and picked up burgers and hot dogs to grill out. More people from the town showed up to help out, even though most of the work had been done already by the time they arrived. Instead, they all gathered on his deck and drank beer and ate food that everyone brought along with them.

By evening, the party had grown so big that it had spilled into the house, filling up his kitchen, living room, and dining room in addition to the deck.

He'd never had this many people in his place before. He didn't even know this many people. But everyone seemed to know Bella.

He watched her laugh and joke with everyone as she walked through the crowded rooms. He kept a close eye on her. If he was being honest, it was because she'd changed into one of those flowing dresses she'd purchased at Serenity's Attic. The dress was tight around her breasts and stomach then flowed loose around her legs with a sexy little slit up one side, giving him a pretty view of her tan legs every now and then.

She'd tied her long hair in a sexy messy bun at the nape of her neck, which only made him want to untangle it with his hands and lick his way up to her mouth.

The more he watched her, the more he realized he was lucky she hadn't left him after his confession last night. It was true, he still struggled with guilt over Kelly's death. It was also true that, as an adult, he knew there was nothing he could have done back then to stop the events from unfolding. If Elijah Adams hadn't kidnapped Kelly that day, he would have found another opening and gotten her eventually. He'd confessed to stalking the family after seeing Kelly while he'd been painting her room.

His parents had let their daughter's murderer into their home. Into Kelly's room. The fact that a twelve-year-old boy was left to watch his little sister had been the perfect opportunity for the killer to strike.

He'd tried to talk to his parents about it once, and the fight that had ensued convinced him to never bring up the subject again. He even kept quiet on the subject with his brother James.

As far as he was concerned, he had no family. It was one of the reasons he'd been thankful Ben had offered him the job at the resort. He'd been in a bad spot with his family since he'd lost the last fight that he'd had with them over his career choices.

He was finally someplace they couldn't touch him. Independent and free of their reach.

"You're deep in thought," Bella said, walking into his arms while she held a glass of wine.

He smiled down at her. "Just thinking how lucky I am to have you and all these friends." He motioned around the room with his half-empty beer.

"Do you know everyone here?" she asked with a whisper.

He chuckled and leaned closer to her. "I thought you knew everyone."

She smiled and then leaned up and kissed him. "It's like

high school all over again." She sighed. "I told a friend that my parents were going out of town one weekend." She shook her head. "Two hundred kids showed up at my house, dragging kegs and booze of every type. When the police showed up…" She rolled her eyes. "Well, let's say that was one of the darkest days in my past." She tilted her head as if she were thinking. "I think that's when they started threatening to send me to the boarding school."

He smiled down at her. "I'm thankful Ben rescued us both then." He waved his beer towards her brother, who was currently wrestling with his oldest daughter on the living room rug. Sarah had picked up the girls when they'd gone out to pick up the burgers since her mother had had a yoga class to teach later that night.

She followed his gaze and nodded. "I don't know what I would do if he wasn't there to buffer my parents." She turned to him. "You know, that's not a bad idea. We could always throw Ben at your parents."

He laughed and hugged her. "Not a bad idea," he agreed.

"So," she said quietly, "how do we kick everyone out of here?" She wiggled her eyebrows as she ran her hands up his chest.

Ten minutes later, the house was empty, except for Ben, who was trying to gather up his daughter's toys from the living room floor while Bella and Sarah chatted.

"Thanks for all the help today." He shook the man's hand when he threw a massive bag over his shoulder filled with the toys and other kid things.

"Any time." Ben smiled at him, then leaned in close. "Sarah told me that Bella knows about Kelly." His friend frowned slightly. "If you need me to talk to her…"

"No," Calvin jumped in. "I think we got it all out in the open."

"Good." Ben slapped him on the shoulder.

He chuckled. "She thinks I need to hire you as a mediator between me and the folks."

Ben laughed and shook his head. "I've met your parents. I don't think even I can convince them of anything they don't want to believe."

Calvin sighed. "Right." He glanced over to Bella. "I told her I loved her," he said, catching Ben off guard.

"Bout time," he said when he recovered. "Dude, it's been on your face since she stepped off the boat." Ben shook his head. "Kind of like how I felt about Sarah." His smile grew. "One look at her"—his voice rose slightly— "and I fell at her feet."

"Passed out, you mean," Sarah said with a chuckle.

He'd heard the story many times of how Ben had arrived at the resort to assess Sarah for her long-lost grandfather, who owned the place and was ready to hand it and Elite Resorts International, his other business, over to his only grandchild. Ben had been fighting the flu and had passed out cold at Sarah's feet.

"Get new jokes," Bella said, rolling her eyes.

"We do. We have you living in town now," Ben said, walking over and kissing his sister's forehead. Then his smile fell away. "Don't scare us like this again."

"The security system is in place now." She hugged her brother, then kissed each of her nieces. "Thanks for helping today."

"Any time," Ben added and took a sleepy child from Bella.

They watched them drive away, then he shut and locked the door and walked over to the security panel.

He showed her the system. "Here's the code." He punched it in, and the system turned green. It showed all the windows and doors in the house as green dots on a flat screen. "We can go over it in more detail tomorrow, but for now…" He turned to her and took her mouth. He'd been starved for the taste of her again.

"Do you have a full week off from work?" she asked with a sigh.

"Yes." He smiled down at her.

"Good." She sidestepped him and walked over to the countertop. "Then you can go with me to LA on Friday."

His steps faltered as he made his way towards her. "Friday?" he asked, suddenly remembering that she'd mentioned she had commitments at the end of the week.

"Yes, I have this gala I'm..." she started to say, moving around the island as he stalked her. He laughed and half chased her as she tried to finish talking. "I'm supposed to..." She raced out of his hold with a giggle. "Black tie..."

He wasn't paying much attention, and when he finally caught her, he pulled her up to sit on the edge of the counter and he kissed her. Her legs wrapped around him as his hands traveled up her silky-smooth legs to find her wet under her panties.

"My god," he groaned, needing to feel more of her. "I don't think I can wait," he said against her neck.

"No, don't." She urged him on.

He bent down as pulled the skirt up high over her thighs. He had a moment to register soft white lace before he pulled it aside and laid his mouth over her pussy, licking and kissing her until her knees tightened on his shoulders. Her fingernails dug into his shoulders as he slid a finger into her heat.

"Calvin," she cried out as she arched for him.

She tasted so good that he didn't think he could ever get his fill of her.

"That's it, come for me, Bella," he urged her as his hand traveled higher under the dress and gripped her hips.

"Calvin, I can't... please..." she begged him.

She tugged and pulled him until he stood between her

legs, using his thighs to spread her legs wider. He pulled on a condom and slid slowly into her.

"I love you, Bella," he said as he kissed her.

She smiled at him and then held on as he showed her exactly what she did to him.

When he carried her upstairs a few minutes later, she was lax in his arms and humming a song.

"That's nice," he said as he laid her on the bed and helped her out of the dress. "What's it called?"

She stilled and then laughed. "Leave it to me to date a man who doesn't know my number-one hit."

He flushed and avoided her eyes. "I…" he started to say, but she stopped him.

"No, don't. It's okay." She smiled. "I don't expect everyone to listen to my songs." She pulled off the dress and tossed it aside.

He picked it off the floor and hung it in the closet, then double-checked the sliding doors. He pulled the blinds shut as she pulled on one of his T-shirts and her sleeping shorts, the really small ones he liked with the hearts and flowers. His eyes moved back up to hers when he realized she'd been saying something.

"Sorry, what?" He shook his head clear of the image of him taking her again. Peeling off those shorts and…

"Earth to Calvin." She snapped her fingers and laughed.

"Sorry, I just have to…" He picked her up and kissed her. She wrapped her legs around his hips and held on as he pressed his hard-on against her core. God, he wanted her again. He would always want her again.

He laid her down on the edge of the bed, and she began to move under him, and he knew that there wouldn't be a time he didn't want her as much as he did now.

When he pulled the comforter over them both, they were both still naked.

"Is that how you're going to distract me from talking about my work each time?" She giggled against his chest.

He sighed. "Sorry, you were just very distracting in that dress today. Then it was those shorts…" He closed his eyes, trying to will his body to shut down instead of heat up for her again.

He felt her sigh as she ran her fingertips over his chest in little patterns.

"So, you'll go with me to LA on Friday?" she asked.

He thought about it, then nodded. "What kind of gala did you say this was?"

"Black tie." She leaned up and looked down at him. "You'll need a tux," she said with a frown.

"I've got one. I need it sometimes for work."

"Right." She rested her chin on her fist, which rested in the middle of his chest. "Good."

"How long do we have to be out there?"

"You? As long as you want before you have to go back to work. Me?" She frowned. "Maggie texted me that my last commitment will end in September." She frowned. "Which means, I won't be able to move out here until fall."

He sat up a little, pulling her with him. "September?" He frowned.

She nodded and laid her head against his chest. "You won't change your mind about this, about us, if I'm away for two months, will you?"

He shook his head. "That's not what I'm worried about," he explained, thinking about the crazy person or persons that had it out for her.

She glanced up at him. "If Michael and everyone in Hollywood sees you and I together…"

"You think he'll stop?" he asked. He doubted it but didn't want to keep her up all night. Instead, he pulled her back down and held her against his chest.

"I can only hope," she said with a yawn.

"I'll arrange our flights tomorrow," he replied and listened as she fell asleep. Nothing would change his mind about wanting her right where she was. He was a better person with her around. A complete person. She was the only family he needed.

CHAPTER TWENTY-THREE

Calvin filled the following day with fun things and some local events. They went blueberry picking in the morning across the county line at a farm they purchased local produce from. Then he took her to a small winery for lunch and a wine tasting event.

Then he took her out in the sailboat again. This time, he opened the sail while she stood at the helm and steered into the sunset. She realized once he threw the anchor down in the middle of a small inlet that she hadn't gotten woozy even once.

He'd packed snacks. Not as elaborate as the ones Adam had brought that first trip, but still, the cheese and crackers with fresh fruit were perfect with the bottle of wine he'd purchased from the winery earlier.

As they started heading back to the docks around sunset, she realized that she could get used to being spoiled by him.

She helped him secure the sailboat and even helped him clean it before heading into town for dinner.

As with each time she moved around town, she ran into

people she knew. This time, it was a couple of school friends that had gone to Brighton.

She tried to discourage them from taking up too much of her time, since she wanted to enjoy a quiet dinner with Calvin, but he'd been pulled in the opposite direction when he ran into a few co-workers. She found herself at the bar talking to Robin and Cindy, two of her closest friends from school, while Calvin stood at the other end of the bar talking to two guys she'd seen at the resort.

Her eyes kept darting up to him, across the bar, and each time their eyes would connect, she'd smile at him. He would give her these sexy looks that had her knees growing weak.

By the time their name was called for a table, he had found his way over to her. She quickly introduced him to her friends before they sat down in a booth near the back wall.

"Is this place always this crazy?" she asked when they were alone.

"No, they have a school reunion this weekend at the high school. I think a lot of these people are in town for that," Calvin answered.

After ordering a bottle of wine, they ordered dinner and talked about their days in school. Calvin seemed really interested in her time at Brighton. He told her that Ben had enjoyed his two years working there as dean when she'd been attending classes. Bella knew that once they'd had the girls, he had decided he needed more time at home. Besides, running both businesses was plenty enough for them to handle while chasing two little ones.

"So, are you nervous about the interview tomorrow?" he asked shortly after their food was delivered.

She set her fork down and frowned. "I wasn't until you mentioned it."

When she noticed the frown spread on his lips, she laughed and picked up her fork again. "Relax." She chuckled.

"I was just joking." He looked slightly relieved. "Not really. I've done enough interviews over the past few years that it's like flying now. You always have some nerves, but at this point, I can work through them."

He nodded. "I'll wager that this interview is a little different than any you've done in the past."

"True." She glanced around the room as she thought of the possible questions that would be thrown at her. Her eyes fell on a dark-haired man at the end of the bar who was staring at her. She felt a shiver race up her spine as he lifted a beer and saluted her. It wasn't the move so much, but the look he was giving her that had her turning her back on the man and focusing on Calvin as he talked about all the preparations for the interview.

By the following morning, she felt the butterflies in her stomach as she sat across from a row of cameras. It was easily one of the most nerve-wracking things Bella had ever had to do. She assumed because this mattered more than all the other interviews. She'd taken almost a full hour in makeup and had spent about that same amount of time picking out the right outfit for the interview.

They'd decided to set up the shoot outside on the wide back porch that overlooked the sound and green yard of the resort, and Calvin stood against the railing.

When the cameras started, a few lighthearted questions were tossed at her. Maggie had given her several talking points to discuss, things like her upcoming album and events she would be attending that weekend.

As she talked about these simple things, she relaxed and almost forgot why they were there in the first place. Then the questions started coming at her about Michael Himes. She tried not to show the tension as it crept into her, but when the reporter straight up asked her if she was stalking him, she had to take several breaths before answering.

"My commitments with Mr. Himes were nothing but professional. I agreed to go with him to the opening of *Rivers Crossing* to promote "Someday Hope," which had been selected for the soundtrack. I'm very thankful to the director and his team for choosing my number-one hit to represent their movie." She smiled and tried to represent ease in her demeanor. "However, the facts are, I have never pursued a personal relationship with Mr. Himes and have warded off any advances he has made towards me. Unfortunately, because of some recent… trouble that has befallen me, my agent and the good people at the Silver Cove police force have all agreed that it was best for me to put out a restraining order on Mr. Himes."

"So, you did put a restraining order on Michael Himes?" the reporter asked.

"Yes."

"Can you tell us more about what events you're talking about that led you to such drastic measures?"

"My apartment in LA was broken into, then my rooms here at the resort were destroyed. I've even had credible threatening messages left on—"

"By Mr. Himes himself?" the woman broke in and asked, looking a little put back.

"They were sent from a burner phone. The police are looking into—"

"So, you have no proof they were sent by Michael Himes?"

"No," she answered with a slight smile. "The police seem to think—"

The woman's eyebrows shot up. "They said the threats and the break-ins were Michael Himes?"

"N-no," she stuttered as she took a deep breath, trying to calm her heart rate down. "They are still looking into where the threats have come from. My agent believed it was the best course of action after his latest lie-riddled interview."

The reporter tilted her head slightly as her eyes moved past Bella to land on Calvin. "I see that your mystery man, who we now know is Calvin Winters, is here. Is it true that he works for your brother's business, East Haven Resorts? The place in which you are staying?"

"Yes." She smiled over at Calvin; he was frowning at the back of the reporter's head since she'd turned back towards Bella. "Calvin is an old friend of the family."

"And you were aware of his dark past?" The woman's smile turned sinister.

"I am. No child should ever have to lose a family member to a psychopath. The fact that his five-year-old sister was snatched from her own yard while his parents weren't home is devastating." She straightened her shoulders. "No child should ever be blamed for matters that were out of their hands."

"So, you know that at one point, Calvin was dragged down to the police station and questioned as a suspect?"

Bella's eyes narrowed. "Yes, I believe the police were just doing their job and trying to find Kelly Winters. Unfortunately, Calvin was twelve at the time. Even their parents were questioned, and they had been having lunch at their country club when Kelly was snatched. The real killer, Elijah Adams, is spending life behind bars thanks to DNA found at the scene. The man had been hired by Calvin's parents to paint Kelly's room. He'd stalked the little girl and chose a time when she was most vulnerable. It's unfortunate." Her eyes moved over to Calvin's. "The man left the family shattered and broken in more ways than one."

The woman shifted some papers in her hands and cleared her throat, and Bella could tell that she was growing agitated that the line of questioning hadn't resulted in the drama she'd hoped for.

From there, the questions returned to her music and if she'd be returning to Hollywood.

After the cameras were shut off, the reporter thanked her, and Bella stood back as everything was put away and carted towards the ferry.

"That was intense," Calvin said, running his hands up and down her arms.

"I'm sorry about the personal questions about you. I should have warned you that I thought it was a possibility," Bella said to him.

He smiled down at her. "I figured it could be, with me standing five feet away."

"Do you think that will send a clear message to Michael?" she asked as the ferry left the docks.

"If not, I don't know what else could." He sighed before leaning down and kissing her.

Two days later, they stepped off the plane in LA. The entire trip was less nerve-racking with Calvin by her side. Somehow, everything she did with him was easier and more fun. The long plane ride seemed to fly by quickly, as opposed to the one she'd taken out to Maine by herself less than three weeks ago.

As they waited for their luggage to arrive, a swarm of reporters flooded around them, screaming questions at them. It took two security guards to clear a path so they could finally get their luggage and head towards the doors to catch a ride to her apartment.

Then one question thrown at them made her stop and turn towards the group.

"What are your thoughts about Michael Himes lawsuit against you?" someone shouted at her.

"Sorry?" she asked the male reporter who'd shoved a

microphone in her face. "What lawsuit?"

"You didn't know about the legal action the award-winning director has threatened to file against you for defamation?" the man asked.

"No," she answered and turned to push their way to the string of waiting taxis.

When they were in a car, heading towards her place, she pulled out her cell phone and called Maggie.

"What's this about Michael suing me?" she asked when her agent answered the phone.

"What?" Maggie asked. "When?"

"I don't know. Apparently, the press already knows about it." She leaned her head back and closed her eyes.

"I'll call you back," Maggie said before hanging up.

"You okay?" Calvin asked.

"How can he sue me?" She groaned.

"Hey, whatever it is, we'll deal with it." He had taken her hands in his and was rubbing his thumb over the insides of her palm.

"I know, it's just... why can't the man leave me alone?"

"Good question. I may just have to have a one on one with the man."

"Don't you dare." She sat up and turned towards him. "That's all we need is you getting into a fistfight with him. Can you imagine the lawsuit then?"

He chuckled. "I wouldn't..." Then his eyebrows shot up slowly. "Okay, maybe I would." He laughed and kissed her. "For you, I'm willing to overlook it."

"Thanks." She rolled her eyes.

By the time the taxi arrived at her apartment complex, she was exhausted and thankful the event wasn't until tomorrow night.

"I'm planning on sleeping until noon," she said as Calvin

helped cart their luggage out of the back of the taxi and tipped the driver.

One of the security members of her building rushed to help them carry in the bags.

"Good to have you back, Miss Rothschild," the man said as he shifted her bags under his arm.

"Thanks, Kenny." She smiled at the older man. "Kenny, this is Calvin. He'll be staying with me for a while." The man nodded his welcome. "Is everything okay? Did the police finish up their... with everything?"

"Yes, ma'am. They've come and gone. They left last week sometime. The place has been quiet since then," Kenny responded.

"Thank you," she said as the elevator doors slid open.

Stepping into her apartment for the first time in over a month, she felt oddly empty as she looked around. It no longer felt like her home. Even her furniture, although nice, just wasn't to her tastes anymore. Instead of the shiny new expensive items, she longed for worn and comfortable things surrounding her.

"Nice place," Calvin said beside her.

"It was home." She turned to him and wrapped her arms around him. "Now you are," she said before kissing him.

They ordered Chinese delivery since her fridge and cupboards were bare. By the time their food arrived, Maggie had called her back.

"So?" she asked as Calvin set the food out on the kitchen table. "Is it true?"

"Apparently, he didn't like some of the things you said during your interview." Maggie chuckled. "He's threatened to sue, but so far, he hasn't. I don't think he has a leg to stand on, since he did his interview first and slandered you first. I think they're just empty threats."

Bella relaxed. "What's his deal?" she asked as she dished

up some chow mein. "Why is he so obsessed with me? I thought he'd moved on. Wasn't he seen with a few other actresses while I was away?"

"Several," Maggie answered. "But I think you are the only one who has turned him down."

"Great, just my luck." Bella rolled her eyes and smiled at Calvin. "My taste in men does not include sniveling directors who throw fits when they don't get what they want, then set out to ruin people who don't like him."

Maggie chuckled. "Is your man with you?"

"Calvin," she supplied with a smile. "Yes, we're having Chinese."

"I won't keep you. Tell me the man has a tux and that you'll be at your hair and makeup appointment on time tomorrow."

"He does and I will."

"Good, now get some rest. You can't have dark circles under your eyes for the award ceremony. I mean sleep, sleep and not sexy playtime with Mr. Tall and Hunky." Maggie chuckled.

"Yes, Mom," Bella said before hanging up.

CHAPTER TWENTY-FOUR

Calvin stood in complete shock as Bella walked out of the bedroom. He'd pulled on his tuxedo and had been waiting for the limo that Maggie had sent for them to arrive. But when he turned to see Bella walking towards him in a sexy silver number, he was pretty sure every part of his body hardened.

"Well?" she asked as she did a little turn. The back of the silver dress exposed her entire back with only a few thin strips of material that crossed her shoulders.

The silver shimmered in the light, highlighting her soft curves. Long dangly earrings swayed as she turned. They matched a long silver chain filled with diamonds wrapped around her neck and several bracelets that traveled up her arm like a choker.

She'd gone to a hair appointment earlier and had come back with her long hair twisted up in an elaborate knot.

Walking over, he reached out to touch her, then pulled his hands back. He didn't want to mess her up. Not when she was looking so perfect.

"You look… amazing," he said, a little breathless.

"Thank you." She ran her eyes up and down him. "Wow, you look even sexier in a tux."

He chuckled and then held out his hand. "The car is here." He motioned towards the door. "Shall we?"

She nodded and they walked out.

When they slid into the car, he turned to her.

"I guess I don't even know what kind of event this is tonight," he said as the car started moving.

"It's an award ceremony." She smiled at him. "I'm up for best new artist."

"You are?" He felt guilty that he hadn't asked before. "Wow, I should've known."

She chuckled. "I'm glad you didn't. I feel less nervous because of the lack of pressure." She took several deep breaths.

"Okay, then I'll just pretend this is a standard date." He smiled as he picked up her hand and lifted it to his lips. "Are these real?" He frowned at the chain of diamonds.

"They're on loan," she said with a chuckle. "Don't worry, they go back to the jeweler's tomorrow morning."

"Great." He swallowed and tried to imagine how much the jewelry she was currently wearing was worth.

"I'd warn you about this," she said as the limo slowed down, "but there really isn't anything I could tell you that would prepare you for what's about to happen." She smiled. "Just smile and nod. By the way…" Her eyes ran up and down him. "You look damn sexy in a tux."

He hadn't expected the onslaught of flashes the moment he helped Bella out of the limo. Nor had he expected questions to be shouted at them as they called their names over and over again.

He did what she'd suggested as Bella hung on his arm while they followed the carpet towards the front doors of the theater. She stopped a few times and took questions from some of the media. He was even asked a few questions and responded with short answers.

"You did well," she said when they stepped inside.

"Is it always like that?" he asked, glancing over his shoulder as the door closed.

She chuckled and held onto him even more. "Sometimes it's worse. We rushed through there pretty quickly."

"Sorry." He realized he'd been leading her across the space quickly.

"No, it was perfect." She smiled. "I didn't want to answer too many questions."

Her smile fell away as she glanced over his shoulder. He felt her tense and instantly shifted around to see what had caused her eyes to go dark.

He'd seen the man on the interview he'd given before Bella's and knew Michael Himes instantly as he walked across the room towards him. Stepping in front of Bella, he stopped the man from approaching her.

"I'm sorry," he said easily, "Bella doesn't wish to speak to you."

The man's eyes ran up and down him like he was nothing more than an annoyance.

"She'll make time for me if she knows what's good for her career," the man said, trying to shove past him.

Calvin held firm. Even though the man had more bulk than he did, Calvin bet he had more muscle.

"That's fine, I'm sure there are some police around here." He looked around. "To see to hauling you in for breaking the restraining order she has out against you." He leaned closer to the man and lowered his tone. "Not to mention all the reporters out there that would love to hear how you just threatened her career while they snapped pictures of you being hauled away in handcuffs."

"No one would dare." The man's chest puffed out. "I'm a legend in this town."

Calvin chuckled. "Call yourself whatever you want. Bella wants nothing to do with you. Ever again. If you keep insisting, you'll have to go through me first." He took Bella's hand in his and walked with her down the hallway.

"That was… amazing," she said as they entered the main theater. She tugged him to a stop then wrapped her arms around him and leaned up to kiss him. "Thank you."

He relaxed a little as his hands moved to her hips. He'd wanted to say more to the man, to do more, but he'd heard a few camera shutters around them and knew that if he crossed the line, he'd be the one being hauled away.

"By tomorrow, that will be all over the news," she said, taking his hand and making their way towards their seats.

"I couldn't let him get close to you. The man's an ass," he said under his breath.

"Tell me about it." She chuckled as they were shown their seats.

"What happens now?" he asked after sitting down. The seats around them were still empty but the room was filling up quickly.

"Now, we sit back and enjoy the show." She shrugged as she straightened her dress.

"When will you know if you won?" he asked, glancing around and spotting some of his favorite artists. He'd never been one to get weird when seeing or meeting famous people. After all, the resort had its fair share of them coming in as guests.

"When they get to the best new artist part. If they call my name." She smiled. She leaned closer to him and whispered. "Which I'm seriously hoping they will."

"Who are you up against?"

She handed him a program and pointed to the short list.

He whistled lightly. "Heavy hitters." He glanced at her sideways. "You have this in the bag."

She chuckled. "I'd be happy to win, but I'm just honored to be nominated."

He laughed. "Isn't that what you told the press?" She nudged his shoulder playfully. "Do you have your acceptance speech?"

She nodded and pulled out a small card from her purse.

"Can I see…" He reached for it, but she yanked it away and stuffed it back in her purse.

"No." She shook her head. "It's bad luck."

He chuckled and took her hand in his. "For good luck." Then he raised her fingers to his lips.

Just then, a photographer stopped in front of them and snapped the picture. "Wonderful shot." The woman smiled down at them. "Want me to send you this?" she asked Bella.

Bella chuckled and nodded. "That would be great." Bella gave her the contact information for her agent.

"Smart," he said when they were alone again.

"Hm?"

"Not giving out your personal information."

"Never." She frowned slightly. "I learned that lesson. "Maggie has agreed to vet all future contacts I have."

"Good." He nodded.

"It's what I pay her for." She smiled. Just then, the seats next to theirs were filled and their chance to have a private conversation was taken away from them as the rows started to fill more quickly.

When the lights dimmed, Calvin sat back and enjoyed the show.

The closer they got to her category, the more nervous he could tell she was feeling. She reached over and took his hand and, when her name was finally called, along with the rest in her category, she squeezed his hand as the camera focused on her face.

He was there to hold her hand when someone else's name was called. Leaning closer to her, he whispered he was sorry she didn't win.

She smiled over at him and nodded. "I was prepared for it." She sighed.

He could tell she was sad, but then he leaned over and kissed her, and he felt her melt next to him.

"When can we leave?" he asked.

She chuckled. "During the next break."

They made their way out of the theater when the cameras went dark and guests stood up to use the bathroom or chat.

He made a point to stay focused on the door and not let any reporters or guests distract them as they headed outside.

When the fresh air hit them, more cameras were shoved in their face.

He tried to block them, but she touched his arm lightly and he stepped aside while she gave a short little speech about being thankful that she'd been nominated, and that the other artist deserved to win.

When they finally made it into the back of the limo, he pulled her into his arms and held her, thinking that she would cry. Instead, her hands started running under his jacket.

"Bella?" He closed his eyes and enjoyed the smell of her skin.

"I don't want to think about losing. Help me forget it. Let me just..." She ran her mouth over his jawline.

He didn't need any more encouragement. His hands started roaming over the silver dress. When his fingers touched bare skin, he groaned. "Nothing matters as much as this. As much as you," he said as he trailed his mouth down her neck. When he reached the chain of diamonds, he stilled and realized the car had slowed.

Glancing around, he noticed they were less than a block from her place. Taking a few deep breaths, he held onto her until it stopped in front of her building.

Taking her hand, he helped her out of the car and started towards the front doors. Kenny opened the glass door and stood back to let them pass by. Just as they did, the door shattered in the man's hands. Bella screamed and he pulled her forward as he covered her body with his.

He lay on top of her on the cement out front of her building as he heard more shots bounce off the cement tiles inches from them. He pulled her through the glass shards while Kenny lay on the sidewalk bleeding and staring up into the sky.

Once he was sure they were safely shielded, he pulled out his phone and dialed 911 as his eyes ran over Bella.

She had a few cuts on her hands and knees from the glass or the pavement, but otherwise she appeared to be unharmed as she held onto him.

"Kenny," she said, starting to move towards the doorway.

"No." He held her still and then gave the dispatcher the information she needed.

"Calvin, let me go. Kenny's hurt." She tried again to pull away.

"Sweetie, there's nothing we can do for him now." He held onto her when she buried her face into his chest. He'd seen the man's eyes staring blankly as he'd shielded Bella from the bullets.

"Kenny?" She cried into his chest. "Why?"

Another man dressed in the building security uniform rushed out of the elevator and headed towards them.

"Are you hurt?" The man knelt beside them. From this

angle, they could only see the broken glass covering the lobby floor.

"Steve," Bella cried. "Kenny." She pointed towards the door. "He's been shot."

The man pulled out a walkie talkie and rushed through the opening where the glass door used to be.

Calvin was about to warn him that there might still be an active shooter, but less than a minute later, he came back inside, blood covering his hands and a look on his face that assured them that it was too late for Kenny.

Bella turned and cried into Calvin's chest again.

"Bella, my god." He closed his eyes as thoughts of what might have happened if Kenny hadn't rushed to open the door and stepped in front of Bella. "Are you hurt?" he asked when he felt her shaking.

"No, just some cuts," she said between sobs. "What happened?" She blinked up at him a few times.

Even though there hadn't been any real loud sounds, he'd known instantly that they were shots. The streets had just been too loud to hear the faint popping sounds. He'd been to the shooting range enough to know the damage a bullet could do.

"Someone shot at us." He pulled her up to her feet and ran his eyes and his hands over her, making sure she wasn't injured past a few cuts and scrapes.

"Are you hurt?" she asked him, doing the same.

When her hands came away bloody, he cursed as the sting in his arm finally registered.

"Calvin, you've been shot!" she cried out, and rushed to remove his jacket.

He looked down at his ruined coat and sighed as she tossed it aside. "Now I'll need a new tux," he said as she pushed him to sit on a bench.

Seeing the bloody shirt sleeve as she pushed it off him, he winced at the sting of his skin sticking to the wet material.

He intuitively knew it was nothing more than a scrape, but still she worried over him until the paramedics arrived and took over. She'd held his ruined shirt against the cut and cried.

"Bella, it's just a nick," he assured her. "I could've cut it on the glass." He motioned to the door. "Or the metal rim of the door." He noticed a jagged piece of metal still holding a shard of glass where he'd dragged her through moments ago.

The police were buzzing around as the paramedics bandaged up his arm.

He didn't want Bella to see Kenny, so he kept them inside the building. When he could, he asked about the man and was told Kenny had taken two bullets, one to the chest and the other through the neck. He'd most likely died instantly.

When Calvin's phone rang, he pulled it out of his ruined jacket and, upon seeing Ben's face, groaned and answered the call.

"What the hell. Did you just get shot?" Ben barked at him.

CHAPTER TWENTY-FIVE

Bella couldn't get warm. Even though she sat in her apartment, covered in a thick blanket, wearing her thickest sweats and heaviest socks, she was still shivering.

Calvin was back on the phone after having changed from his ruined tux, pacing the floor of her apartment.

"I don't give a damn," he said, and then turned his eyes towards her. "It's obvious who it was aimed at…" He waited and listened again as she laid her head back against the sofa.

Images of the last moments of Kenny's life flashed behind her eyelids each time she closed them. So, she opened them again and looked at her ceiling.

"Yeah." Calvin groaned and hung up. "The police are sending…" He sighed when his phone rang again. "It's your brother again." He rolled his eyes and answered the call. "She's resting," he answered. "She's showered, changed, and sitting on the sofa safe and sound." Calvin listened for a moment, then held out his phone for her to take.

"Hi," she said, her voice sounding as if it was miles away, like she was stuck in a tunnel.

"Are you okay?" Her brother's voice was soothing, and she closed her eyes again.

"I am," she said, her voice shaking. "Calvin is the one who got shot," she reminded him.

"He says it was a scrape he got from the glass."

Her eyes opened and landed on Calvin, who was still standing over her. "He's lying," she said with a slight smile, which Calvin returned.

"I'm sorry about your doorman," Ben said softly, then he covered the phone as she listened to Sarah tell him something. "Sarah wants me to ask if you've eaten anything. She says shock can cause you to blow through..." Her brother muffled the phone, but she heard him question his wife. "Seriously? That's what you wanted to ask her?"

"Ben?" She waited until her brother got back on the phone. "I'm fine. We're both fine. We ordered delivery. It should be here soon." She glanced over at Calvin, and he looked down at his watch. "The police agreed to send someone over to keep an eye out," she said. Calvin nodded and held up two fingers. "Two cops."

"I wish you'd never left Silver Cove," Ben said with a sigh.

"That makes two of us." She rested back again.

"So, you're coming back then?" Ben asked.

"Yes, at the end of—"

"No, I mean, you're hopping on a plane tomorrow," her brother broke in. "There is no way I'm letting you stay out there now."

She chuckled slightly. "This is my home, until I move in September."

"To hell with—" Suddenly, the phone was grabbed, and Sarah's voice came on the line.

"Hi, sweetie, how are you?" her sister-in-law asked in a calm voice.

"I'm good," she answered with a sigh.

"Bella, we think it's best that you come back here. Cancel your commitments. It's obvious that the person… well, he's willing to go to great lengths to get at you and, now, he won't even stop at murder."

Bella shivered and pulled the blanket closer to her.

"I can't bring this to you." She closed her eyes as more tears rolled down her cheeks. "Kenny, he was… a friend. If it had been you or Ben or, god forbid, one of the girls…" Her breath hitched. "I'd never forgiven myself."

Sarah was quiet for a moment. "I can't say the same thought hadn't crossed our minds, but we're family. We've got your back. Besides, if anyone snoops around Silver Cove, they're bound to stand out. There in the city, well, this is just another Saturday night shooting."

Bella knew Sarah was right. It was a lot harder to get away with things in a small town. But someone had broken into her rooms at the resort and at Calvin's place without any witnesses. How safe could she really be anywhere? At least here in the city, she had a full force of police to protect her now that they'd agreed to put someone on her full time. At least, that's what Calvin had been arguing to get for almost half an hour.

"One month," she said, suddenly. "The end of July. I promise…"

Suddenly Sarah was gone, and Ben was back. "Fine, then tell Calvin not to leave your side until you get back here. I'm holding him personally responsible to make sure you get home safe."

She looked up at Calvin. "His job—"

"Is secure," Ben said. "Just make sure you are. I trust him." Ben sighed. "He's the only one I trust with my sister."

Since Calvin had been standing directly in front of her and her brother's voice echoed, Calvin smiled.

She reached up and handed the phone back to him.

"I'm on it," Calvin said with a smile, then he laughed at something her brother said to him before hanging up. "He says not to bother him again unless I really get shot and not just scratched."

She frowned at the white bandage on his lower arm. "You were really shot. The medic said…"

He sat next to her and wrapped his arms around her. "Looks like I'm not leaving your side until we head back home." He glanced down at her. "You okay with this?"

She held onto him and nodded her head, not wanting to let go.

"You're shivering." He pulled back and frowned at her.

"I can't seem to get warm." She tried to hold onto him again.

"Come on," he said as he picked her up. "I could use a shower. A hot one." He carried her into the bedroom but set her down when her doorbell rang. "That'll be the food. Stay put," he warned her, then he disappeared back out front.

When he came back, she was lying on the edge of her bed, half-awake and still very cold.

"The food's in the oven on warm." He picked her up again. "Shower, food, bed. That order." He set her on her feet and started removing the clothes that she'd changed into the moment she'd entered her apartment.

Now, he pulled them off her slowly as the water in her shower heated. When they stepped under the spray together, she melted under the warmth.

"Your bandage," she said sometime later when she felt her bones stop shaking.

"They gave me some extra gauze. I'll cover it again after I'm dry." He held her still in his arms.

"Poor Kenny." She sighed and shut her eyes. "I don't even know if he had a family."

"Divorced, no kids," he answered. "I asked the other security guard."

She nodded. "He was always so nice to me."

"He stepped in front of the bullets," he said and this time she felt him shiver. "I don't even want to think of what could have happened."

"Do you think this was Michael?" she asked.

"Your manager seems to think so. She called when you were changing."

"I didn't think. I should…" She glanced towards the shower doors, but he held her still.

"Later. I told her you were resting and safe," he said. "For now, let's turn everything off." He kissed the top of her head.

She nodded in agreement. "Calvin?" She glanced up at him. "I'm thankful you're okay. I didn't mean to drag you into my mess."

He cupped her face and pushed her wet hair aside. "This is in no way your fault. You didn't drag me. I surrendered to those sexy eyes of yours." He smiled. "And those lips, not to mention those legs."

She laughed and then sighed. "Thank you for being here. For staying with me."

"Hey." He hugged her again as they stood under the spray together. "I'm not complaining. I get a whole month off with pay."

She sighed. "Playing bodyguard to me. Maybe you should have asked for double pay?"

After they stepped out of the shower, she dried off and pulled on the thick sweat suit again. They ate the pizza in her living room and turned on the television when Ben texted them that it was all over the news already.

Sure enough, there was even grainy security footage of the entire incident. She closed her eyes after seeing Kenny's body hit the ground.

"In what's being described as a murder attempt on Bella Rothschild, tonight's drive-by shooting has left Miss Rothschild's doorman, Kenny Morton, a fifty-three-year-old employee at the Stanford Arms Executive Apartments, dead. No word on Miss Rothschild or her date to the Hollywood Highlights Music Awards, Calvin Winters. Miss Rothschild was up for Best New Artist, but at the ceremony lost out to up-and-coming star Cara Knightswood. In a shocking twist shortly after tonight's ceremony, the HHMA committee has come forward and issued a statement that the award was given to Miss Knightswood by mistake. They have released a statement that the award should have gone to Bella Rothschild instead..."

Bella sat up, her heart jumping in her chest. "I won?" She frowned at the screen as the reporter continued to talk about an investigation into why Cara's name was called instead of Bella's. "I won?" she asked again.

"Sounds like you did." Calvin chuckled and turned up the television.

"Speculations are running wild. There are reports claiming that Michael Himes had some pull on the committee and pushed the change at the last minute. Even more speculation is going around about the validity of Miss Rothschild's claims that Michael Himes was the aggressor in their very public feud. This reporter thinks that the police might want to look into why Mr. Himes left the gala tonight shortly after Bella and Calvin were seen leaving the theater."

Calvin lowered the volume. "Well, guess it's all out there now." He turned to her.

She was still staring at the television. Then she turned to him. "I won!" She jumped up and down on her sofa. Calvin laughed with her and joined in the fun.

It took her almost two hours to settle back down. Of course, another call was taken from her brother, but this time it was a congratulatory call. Even her parents called her. They were a little upset that she hadn't called them to let them know that she had been shot at or that she was okay, but still, their main focus had been her big win. She imagined it was one more thing they could brag to all their friends about.

When she finally did fall asleep, her dreams were filled with blood, broken glass, and Kenny's body.

She woke with a start when Calvin shook her, then pulled her close. "It's just a dream," he whispered into her ear.

"Sorry," she mumbled, holding onto him. "I couldn't stop it." She sighed. His arms tightened around her and then he was kissing her, and she forgot everything except him.

"Better?" he asked as his hands moved over her hips, pulling her closer.

"Getting there." She moved until she straddled his hips. Leaning up, she pulled the T-shirt over her head and watched his eyes heat just before his hands cupped her. Rolling her head back, she moaned at the feeling of him touching her.

"Calvin," she sighed. "I love your hands on me."

He leaned up and placed his mouth where his hands had just been. "I love the taste of you," he said, trailing his mouth over her heated skin. "I don't think I'll ever get enough of you."

She smiled into the darkness and held him to her as he teased her skin with his lips.

Then he was spinning them around until he hovered over her. The bed bounced while he pulled her sweats off her legs, then he disappeared beneath the sheets as he kissed his way down to where she wanted him. Where she'd dreamed of him being. When his mouth found her, she cried out and arched her back, needing more.

"Please," she cried out and balled her fists into the sheets.

"Now, I can't wait. I don't want to." She tugged on his shoulders.

She waited as he slid off his shorts, pulled on a condom, and moaned as he entered her slowly. She'd never imagined loving someone as much as she loved Calvin. Just being with him, having him fill her, complete her... As she felt herself build, she sighed and told him once again how she felt. "I love you," she said against his skin.

When she woke, she could hear Calvin talking to someone in the next room. Glancing at her phone, she frowned at the late hour. How had she slept past ten o'clock? She never slept past eight. Getting up, she quickly dressed in dark yoga pants and a long sweater before heading into the next room.

Maggie stood in her kitchen eating a large muffin with a cup of coffee in her other hand.

"There you are." Her manager set the food and drink aside when she saw her and rushed over to her and hugged her. "You worried me."

The large black woman engulfed her in a hug that felt so good, Bella almost cried again.

"I'm okay." She held onto her friend.

"You scared the shit out of me." Maggie leaned back and looked down at her. "Your man here"—Maggie nodded her head towards Calvin, who was standing in the kitchen holding out a fresh mug of coffee towards Bella— "has been keeping me company." Maggie smiled and moaned slightly. "He's even better looking in person," she whispered, but not low enough that Calvin didn't chuckle when he heard it.

"Now." Maggie dropped her arms and picked up her muffin again. "I brought you food." She motioned towards the basket of muffins and fruit. "Oh, and the entire lobby is full of flowers and gifts waiting to be delivered up to you." She set the muffin back down and walked over to a large box sitting at the end of her kitchen table. "And I brought this…" She held out the box as her smile grew.

"What's…" Bella started to ask, but then noticed the HHMA sticker on the side of the box. "My award?" She gasped and lifted the lid.

The silver and glass award sat nestled in black velvet. Pulling it out slowly, she smiled as she held it up to the light. "Oh my…" She hugged it to her chest as she twirled in circles while Calvin and Maggie laughed.

CHAPTER TWENTY-SIX

Over the next few days, the only time they left the apartment was to head to the small coffee shop at the end of the block. Even then, Calvin tucked her body between the building and his. He made her wear a hat and a large jacket as a disguise.

Two undercover police officers followed them, keeping an eye out for Bella. He'd met the woman and man, who were practically camping out in the lobby. The glass door had been replaced and everything was almost back to normal, with the exception of the makeshift memorial set up outside for Kenny. Bella had insisted on hitting the flower shop and laying a large wreath on the spot herself.

He'd grabbed a bunch of flowers as well. After all, he owed the man his and Bella's lives. They'd attended his funeral and had been plastered all over the news the last few days.

The video of him pulling her out of the way and dragging her to safety was everywhere he looked. The hardest part was watching Kenny drop each time. Even though some media sources blurred out his image, Calvin could still remember seeing the man's eyes.

Maggie seemed to visit them every day. Because of her new fame with the award and all the attention the shooting had gained, Bella had several new interviews scheduled for that week.

He didn't like her being out in the open but knew there was no use hiding away forever. Each time they went outside, either the undercover cops or the security company Maggie had hired was right there. Still, he knew that if someone wanted to, nothing would stop the bullets except a body, like they had before.

He sat back and watched her do interviews for a few morning shows. For one of them, she even brought along her award and showed it off.

He enjoyed seeing her get up on stage and sing with the band that she worked with for all her recordings and stage events. He liked the three guys and ended up talking to them backstage while they waited for their segment.

There were pictures of them plastered on every tabloid cover at every checkout stand. He was starting to get used to seeing their faces everywhere they went.

He never left her side and was thankful she seemed to be enjoying his company. Of course, he would have liked to be able to melt into the background so they could go out and do some sightseeing. He'd only been to California a handful of times in his youth.

Before he knew it, two weeks had passed without any further incidents. Even the police were beginning to think that Michael Himes, who had been brought in and questioned, had decided to back off. Even though there was no proof the shooting had been him, the man's career had taken a huge hit.

His interview was scrutinized and picked apart by

experts willing to give their opinions to the highest-paying news source. Bella turned down several interviews about the subject, since Maggie and he agreed that she should try and not put more speculations out there.

The fact was, they had no clue if Michael Himes was behind the shooting or even the break-ins. All they knew was that he had been the one to switch the envelopes at the award ceremony.

One of the judges, Carmen Langdon, stepped forward in an interview and described how Himes promised her a role in his upcoming movie if she would switch the envelopes.

She had told him that it wouldn't take long for them to discover what she'd done, and he promised her that with his power he would protect her. But when the committee started looking at her, Michael denied her version of the story and started claiming that she had switched the names to impress him in hopes that he would boost her career.

The only problem was she had recorded the conversation on her phone since she was worried that he would renege on the deal.

The muffled recording of Michael's empty promises played on television as much as the video of him pulling Bella to safety while Kenny's body dropped beside them.

Since the matter hadn't been a legal issue, Michael's only recourse was to be dropped from the award's committee and banned from any others in Hollywood.

A week after the shooting, Bella's new album hit number one on the charts. They had celebrated by ordering delivery from a restaurant down the street and lighting every candle she had in her apartment. They had even dressed up, with her wearing one of the fancy and sexy outfits she had tucked in her guest closet. Since he hadn't had time to replace the tux, he'd pulled on a dress coat and tie.

Even though they couldn't go out, it was nice pretending

as they had. But at the end of the second week, he could tell she was starting to go stir crazy.

She'd cleaned her place and had started packing up her things and marking which items she would sell or donate and not take with her.

He was surprised that she didn't plan on taking any of her new furniture with the exception of her bed, which they decided would replace the one in his guest bedroom.

"Let's go out," she said midmorning one day. "I have no commitments today." She glanced towards the windows. "It's sunny and I want to feel the fresh air on my face." She walked over to him and wrapped her arms around him. "Let's go for a drive."

He thought about the logistics of it and frowned.

"Don't do that." She shook her head.

"What?"

"Overthink this. I have a car downstairs in the garage. We hop in it, drive out of the city into the hills, and find some little place to have lunch." She leaned up on her toes and kissed him. "Please?"

He couldn't deny her. Not when she practically purred next to him.

"I'll arrange it." He smiled. "Get dressed." He glanced down at her pajama shorts and a tank top and wished that she would've suggested they spend the day in bed instead.

He talked to the private security on duty and informed them that they would be taking a drive, to which they responded that they would follow them in their car. They reassured him that he wouldn't even know they were back there, but as Bella drove out of the city, he found his eyes glued to the side mirror, making sure that they followed along.

It wasn't that Bella was a bad driver... okay, it was. She was more aggressive than drivers in Silver Cove tended to be. He supposed it was needed in the city. When they finally hit the highway, he relaxed a little seeing that the dark SUV was still two cars behind them.

"Everything okay?" Bella asked as she gunned the small sedan and headed towards the hills.

He glanced over and realized that she was thoroughly enjoying herself.

"Yes." He smiled and tried to forget about the security behind them. "Where are we heading to?"

"I thought we'd head to the beach." She smiled over at him.

He'd been so busy worrying about making sure their security hadn't lost them that he didn't even notice which direction they'd been heading.

"The beach sounds fun." He glanced down at the shorts she'd convinced him to put on and realized they were his board shorts. Chuckling, he silently promised himself he'd relax a little and enjoy the day instead of worrying so much.

"Huntington Beach is one of my favorite places." She sighed as she turned off the highway. "Since it's a workday, and school started this week, hopefully it won't be as crowded. We can find a little hut to eat lunch before we hit the sand and the water."

He reached over and took her hand in his. "That sounds wonderful. I've never been to a California beach before."

"You haven't?" She glanced at him.

"No. I went to Disneyland when I was ten. I've been to San Diego a few times on business. But this is my first trip where I could relax."

"Well then, we'll have to show you some more sights before you go," she said and instantly his worry started up again. He wanted to argue that it wasn't safe, but he kept his mouth shut and glanced at the mirror again to make sure the SUV was still back there.

By the time they stepped into the water, he was completely relaxed again. They had found a small food hut to have a few drinks and eat greasy burgers at.

She'd worn a large sun hat and dark glasses with her long hair tied back in a braid and, thankfully, hadn't been recognized once during the meal.

The two security guards sat in the booth across from them. They filled the men in on what their plans were and were assured that they were there for the entire adventure.

Since the men were dressed in jeans and black shirts, he doubted they would spend much time on the beach.

Still, just seeing Bella in the sexy pink swimsuit had all other thoughts fleeing his mind. They played in the surf until she grew tired and they laid out on the large beach towels she'd packed along.

He stayed busy people watching and watching over her and was happy when she fell asleep beside him. When he noticed her skin start to pink, he nudged her to roll over and wrapped his arms around her. She moaned and snuggled into him and he realized that this was easily one of his favorite memories with her.

When she woke, they headed down the coast a little and found a cute town and another beach restaurant to eat dinner at. This time it was steaks and grilled shrimp with wine. The two security guys sat out in their truck and had sandwiches instead.

As they pulled into her parking garage, he felt as if he'd seen enough sights. He was ready to head home in less than a week.

"What about your car?" he asked as she parked in her spot.

She shrugged and shut it off. "I've arranged to have it shipped with the rest of my stuff." She turned to him. "Did you like the beach today?"

"Yes." He touched the end of her braid. "I'm looking forward to getting home though," he admitted.

"So am I." She smiled. "I only have a few more interviews, which shouldn't take more than four days." She frowned slightly. "Five, tops."

He nodded. "I enjoy watching you work."

She laughed. "I guarantee you'll be bored in ten minutes flat."

He pulled her close. "I never get bored watching you," he said before kissing her.

The knock on her window had them both jumping. One of the security guards for the building stood just outside her door.

He rushed to get out and moved over just as she climbed out of the car.

"I thought you should know, a package came for you earlier today shortly after you left. I've called the police," the man said. His name was Derrick, and he had replaced Kenny.

"A package?" Bella asked.

The man looked over to him. "It was… um, leaking a red substance."

Calvin wrapped his arms around Bella and held on as fear and dread overtook him.

"They are upstairs waiting to talk to you both."

"What was in it?" Bella asked.

"I'm not sure. We didn't open it, they did. Then more cops showed up and, well…" He shrugged. "When we saw you pull up on the camera"—he motioned to the parking garage camera— "I came down to give you a heads-up."

"Thanks." Calvin shook the man's hand before he pulled Bella towards the elevator. They rode up in silence and when the doors slid open, Calvin knew instantly that whatever had been mailed to them was serious.

More than half a dozen police stood in the lobby. Some

took pictures while others talked to the other security personnel.

As they stepped out, every eye turned towards Bella.

"Miss Rothschild." An older woman stepped forward and introduced herself as Captain Elizabeth Feller. "Is there someplace we can go?" she asked the building security officer, who quickly showed them to a small office down the hallway. After the three of them were shoved into the small space, with Bella sitting down in one of the chairs while he stood beside her, the captain started explaining. "Today around noon a package arrived for you special delivery. Your building security, per your private security's request, had it waiting for inspection before delivering it up to you. While they waited, someone noticed it was leaking a red substance and called us." The woman shifted gears and glanced towards him. "We've already confirmed both of your schedules with your private security and have tentatively cleared both of you—"

"Cleared us for what?" Calvin broke in and asked.

"Miss Rothschild." The captain glanced back towards Bella. "Can you tell me when was the last time that saw or spoke to Michael Himes?"

Bella gasped and Calvin reached out to touch her shoulder and felt her shake. "What has this got to do with Michael?" she asked, her voice low.

"Please." She held up her hands. "I'll need you both to answer first."

"The night of the awards," Bella blurted out.

"In the lobby before the event," Calvin finished for her.

The captain nodded. "As I said, we've confirmed that already, I just needed to hear it from you." She took a deep breath. "Michael Himes was found murdered in his home shortly after this package was delivered to you."

Bella's eyes closed and she rested her head back against his arm. He swallowed and held his breath.

"It appears that someone has taken it in their hands to send you some of his… parts." Her eyes went to his. He nodded, showing the captain that she'd said enough.

"Bella." He knelt before her and watched her face pale.

Then she was scrambling and thankfully he handed her the waste bin before she lost the dinner they'd enjoyed earlier.

"He's… dead?" she said, her eyes still closed as she wiped her mouth.

"Yes," the captain answered. "We'll need an official statement from both of you, but that can wait until tomorrow." She nodded as one of the other officers stepped into the small space. The man whispered something to her, and she waved him away. "For now, I'll leave you to head up and get some rest. Your place was inspected to ensure your safety."

"You searched her place?" he asked.

The woman narrowed her eyes at him. "No, your security team rushed up there to inspect the place shortly after you returned."

"Thank you." Bella stood up suddenly and gripped his arm. "We will cooperate. What time do you want us?"

"We'll come to you. I understand how volatile things are right now for you. We don't need the press getting wind that we're questioning either of you. Let me make this clear—at this point, neither of you are on the suspect list." Her eyes moved between them.

"Then you must have some evidence?" Calvin asked.

The woman's eyes narrowed again, and he watched the corner of her mouth twitch. He took it as a good sign and nodded quickly.

"Thank you." He shook her hand again and then helped Bella upstairs.

CHAPTER TWENTY-SEVEN

Even though Calvin tried to keep the news from her, she pulled out her cell phone when she locked herself in her bathroom and read the headlines.

"Director Michael Himes' brutal murder" was plastered on every news site.

When she clicked into one article, she read about how the police had been called to her apartment while she'd been out for the day with Calvin and how the police had found Michael Himes' head in a box that someone had sent to her.

She quickly threw up again and decided she didn't need to know any more details. She scrubbed her teeth and washed her face, then answered the tenth call from Maggie since returning to her apartment.

Maggie kept trying to convince Bella to let her come up, but she insisted that she was just going to get some rest.

"I'm fine," she answered the call.

Instead of Maggie's worried voice, a deep male voice whispered in the phone.

"Did you get my present?"

She swallowed and sat on the edge of the bathtub. "Wh-

who is this?" she asked, her voice shaking as much as the rest of her body was.

"I thought torturing you was fun." The voice chuckled. "Until I killed that doorman." A full laugh sounded in her ear, making her entire body shake. "I guess it's true, when you spill blood, it's like a drug. I have a taste of it, now I'm done playing games. When I come for you, nothing will stop me."

When the line went dead, she was frozen in place listening to the emptiness.

A quick loud knock on the bathroom door had her screaming and dropping her phone. Then Calvin was there, holding her and promising her that everything would be okay. She didn't know how he'd gotten in the locked door, but she was grateful for his arms around her.

"He called," she said into his chest as she held onto him.

"Who?" he asked, then he stiffened. "What did he say?"

She quickly relayed the message, then gasped. "He called on Maggie's cell phone." She stood up and looked around for her phone. "He has Maggie."

"I'll call the police." Calvin pulled out his phone.

She stood there and listened to Calvin speak to the captain that had talked to them earlier that day.

Within half hour, a knock sounded on the door and several police officers filled her living room.

Calvin made coffee while she relayed what had happened. They informed her that Maggie was fine and had lost her phone in a restaurant moments before the call was made to her. She was so worried about her agent that an officer was sent to pick her up and bring her back to spend the night in Bella's guest room.

Was the killer stalking her manager now? What did he hope to gain? Maybe another way to get to her? Was she next on his list?

When Maggie walked in the door behind a larger male

officer, Bella wrapped her arms around the woman and cried. "I thought…" she said into the woman's shoulder.

"Shh, honey, I'm right here. I'm okay," Maggie said and then started crying with Bella.

Her apartment was turned into a makeshift operation headquarters. A cup of coffee was handed to her, but since it was now past one in the morning, she sat on the sofa, propped up against Calvin and fell asleep.

When Calvin shifted to answer his phone, she jolted awake.

"Easy, it's your brother." He waved the phone.

She rested back as he handed the phone to her.

"Bella?" Ben's voice sounded even more worried than it had when she'd talked to him shortly after the news broke of Michael's death.

"I'm okay," she sighed. "There are about a dozen police in my apartment." She glanced around and realized some of them had gone and only three were left. "Maggie's here sleeping in my guest room."

She glanced down the hallway where Maggie had disappeared earlier.

"My god, you scared us." Ben sighed. "Let me talk to Calvin."

She yawned and handed the phone over.

She didn't really pay attention to their conversation, since she was still half-asleep, but when she felt Calvin stiffen and sit up, she focused.

"I think you should tell the police here what you just told me," Calvin said and glanced back at her. "Hang on." He stood up and walked over to the officer who had been left in charge after the captain had left hours ago. "Bella's brother has a possible lead." He handed the man the phone.

"Calvin?" Bella stood up and moved over to him.

"Do you remember Eddie Simons?" he asked her.

She thought about it and shook her head no. "No, should I?"

"He worked at the resort. You went to school with him."

"Worked?" She felt her knees go weak.

"Easy, it's not that..." Calvin held her. "He's been MIA since we left. I guess since I've been gone, no one informed Ben that he hadn't shown up for work. They figured the kid had just gotten another job." She relaxed slightly. "Well, when Ben found out yesterday, he did some research. Since he went to Brighton with you..." Bella remembered the guy now. He'd been her waiter that first day she'd arrived and a few times after. A shiver ran up her spine remembering how he'd acted around her. "Ben remembered the kid had been a troublemaker when Ben was dean of the school during that time. Eddie had been valedictorian of your class."

She nodded. "I remember now."

"Well, on a hunch yesterday, after finding out that he'd been MIA, Ben sent Brock over to his parents' place. Since the kid had been working at the resort, he'd mentioned how his folks had been away on vacation. No one seemed to question him. You know how it is... small towns."

She nodded and felt her stomach roll. "And?"

Calvin glanced at the officers as they continued to talk to Ben as they typed the information down.

"Brock found the older folks in the freezer along with Fredrick Stafford. The folks had been dead for around six months and, well, Fredrick disappeared... the day after he got arrested at the resort." Bella's knees folded and Calvin carried her to the sofa. "Easy," he said to her and a glass of water was shoved in her face by the female officer.

"Drink this," she said.

Bella drank it down and closed her eyes. "Why me?" she asked.

"Brock says there was a shrine built for you in his house.

He's infatuated with you. It appears it started back in school. He left notes everywhere about killing his parents because they wouldn't let him go to California to be closer to you." Calvin's hands tightened on hers. "They have proof that he drove out here during the time your place was broken into. But then, he'd gotten a call from his neighbors who were worried about not seeing his folks around. He had to come back to Silver Cove. He got a job at the resort to be close to your brother. They think he killed Stafford out of rage because of that fight you witnessed. We have him. Now we know who he is." He smiled weakly up at her.

She didn't feel any safer now. Instead, she played back all the times she'd talked to him that first week she'd been at the resort. Each time, she had been so focused on Calvin she had barely given the guy any notice.

Then she stilled and gasped. "I've seen him here a few times." She shook her head. "I didn't even…" She closed her eyes. "He has a face that I just… seem to forget."

"Where?" Calvin asked.

She thought about it and tried to remember each time she'd caught the thin, pale-skinned, dark-haired man looking at her. She listed the few places, including the coffee shop down the street.

"So, he's close," the officer said.

"His poor parents," she said when the police got back to work searching for their new target. Calvin's phone was handed back to him and he talked briefly to Ben before hanging up.

"Ben's getting us tickets to head home tomorrow. You can reschedule any interviews." He pulled her into his arms.

She nodded in agreement. "I'm so tired." She sighed. "So weary of running and hiding."

He sighed and glanced over her shoulder. "We're heading in to get some rest. If you hear anything… knock."

The officer nodded her head and waved them off.

She lay on the bed and sighed as he wrapped his arms around her. "Turn it off for a few hours," he told her. "I'm right here."

She slept without dreaming, thankfully. When she woke, Calvin's arms were still wrapped around her, holding her.

"Feel better?" he asked. The fact that he sounded as if he hadn't slept had her glancing at him.

"I do. Did you get any sleep?"

"A few hours," he admitted with a smile. "I could go for some breakfast and coffee."

She nodded and stretched. "Shower, then food."

She could hear Maggie down the hall talking to someone and laughing.

After taking a quick shower and spending a few minutes to fix her hair and makeup, she felt like attacking the day.

When she stepped out into the living room, she hugged Maggie again and took the coffee mug offered and the large bacon-covered donut.

"I had this sexy beast run down and get us some donuts and coffee." Maggie patted the shoulder of the larger officer who had brought her to her apartment yesterday. The man blushed quickly as he laughed.

Bella smiled at how cute the couple looked and instantly could feel the chemistry between the pair. She was happy to think about that while she ate instead of her own problems.

When the donut was gone and the coffee mug was being refilled by Calvin, she asked, "Any news?"

He nodded. "They put out an APB on the guy and found out he'd been staying at a hotel two blocks away from here."

Bella shivered and sipped her coffee to warm up. "Did they get him?"

"No, he gave the officers the slip. Left all his things in the room, though, and they impounded his parents' car, which he drove out here. They also have the gun he used to shoot his parents, Fredrick, Kenny, and Michael." Calvin smiled. "They think it's the only gun he had." He sobered. "There's video from Michael's place of the murder. It confirms that it was Eddie." Calvin put his head in his hands. "I can't believe I hired the psychopath."

Bella touched his face until he looked up at her. "You couldn't have known."

"I should have." He closed his eyes.

"The man is a psychopath. What's the thing everyone says about them? No one who knew them knew the darkness hidden beneath?" She shook her head. "Sure, the guy creeped me out, but I would have never guessed he was capable of cold-blooded murder."

"Right." He nodded. "We're on a flight heading home this evening. Think you can pack?"

She glanced around. "What about…"

"Maggie's going to stay here and make sure everything else of yours gets shipped off. They'll keep the police detail here to watch her until they catch Eddie." He leaned closer and whispered. "I think Maggie and officer Tom there have a thing going." He chuckled.

Bella glanced over and nodded as the couple whispered something to each other. "I think you're right." She smiled. "It would be nice to have something good come out of this mess."

He held onto her. "I've already got something pretty damn good." He kissed her on the top of the head. "What do you say we go pack?"

It was surprisingly easy to pack up her things, despite knowing that she would never return to the apartment.

Maggie helped her toss the rest of her personal things in the empty boxes that would be shipped with the rest of her stuff. She stuffed her suitcases with items that she would be taking home on the plane.

Calvin's suitcase sat filled by the door already. He spent his time out with the police, trying to get any information he could to them about Eddie.

When her room was bare, she glanced around and thought about all the good times she'd had here. Most of the ones that came to her included Calvin.

"I'm going to miss you," Maggie said as she hugged her. "I've arranged for your interviews to be rescheduled at a studio closer to you in New York for next week. I also got you booked to play on a little show. You may have heard of it. *Saturday Night Live?*" She smiled.

Bella squealed and then hugged Maggie again. "I could just kiss you," she said with a smile.

Maggie laughed and held up her hands. "Oh no, I don't go for skinny white girls." Her eyes darted towards the door.

"No." Bella smiled. "I think you like tall, handsome, blue-eyed cops."

Maggie glared at her. "Girl, that man has some lips I'd like to…" She shook her head and smiled. "His body's not too bad either." She laughed and hugged her again.

"Well, you'll have plenty of time with him. Calvin's out there arranging to make sure he's on your security detail."

Maggie chuckled. "I knew I liked your man for a reason." Then she turned towards her. "Be happy."

"I am." Bella smiled.

"I hate that you're going to be so far away from me, but we can make this work. I promise you."

"I know you can do it." She smiled. "I hired the best of the best."

Maggie laughed. "Suck up."

"I learned from the best." She hugged her friend again.

She tried not to cry as they pulled away from her apartment complex for the last time. But tears rolled down her cheeks when she glanced back as they rolled towards the airport.

Then she turned to Calvin and wiped them away.

"You okay?" he asked.

"Better than okay." She smiled. "I'm going home." She took his hand and rested her head on his shoulder.

CHAPTER TWENTY-EIGHT

It was the best thing Bella could have said to him. He'd been worried for so long that she wouldn't want to return with him. Part of him kept telling himself that he didn't deserve her, while other parts kept screaming at him to take what pleasures he could while he could.

When the cab pulled into the airport parking lot, he helped unload all Bella's luggage to the curb. She'd packed as much as she had because it would be two weeks before her stuff would be shipped out to them.

He didn't mind the extra bags he'd put in the back of the cab for her, since they were all being checked in at the curb at the airport.

"I'm going to go check-in." She motioned to the kiosk stations just inside the door while he waited for the baggage claim employee to finish checking in all her luggage.

"Why don't you wait for me?" he suggested, not wanting her to stray too far from him.

"Calvin, it's just a few feet away." She smiled up at him. "We're in a crowded airport," she reminded him. "This way, we can have a little extra time before our flight to get a glass of wine and maybe some dinner."

"Fine." He sighed as he brushed his lips across hers once more. "Stay within sight," he murmured.

"Yes, sir." She stood back and saluted him with a laugh.

"I love you," he said and kissed her again.

She stopped and her smile slipped slightly as she looked into his eyes. "I love you too."

He felt his heart skip and then she moved away, and he was called to move up in line as the employee helped him start to shuffle their bags onto the conveyer belt.

The man had just handed him the last baggage claim ticket when he heard a commotion as people screamed and ran out of the doors less than five feet from him.

"He has a gun!" someone screamed, causing everyone around him to run in the opposite direction or to crouch to the ground.

He froze as his eyes scanned the area that he'd last seen Bella. As he rushed through the doors, he saw Eddie twist Bella's left arm behind her back.

As he rushed towards them, he watched in horror as she fought to escape Eddie's grip on her.

He was less than ten feet from them when Bella finally broke free. But instead of running away, she jerked her body back and flung it at the skinny man, sending them both flying to the ground.

He heard the gun go off just before it was knocked free of Eddie's hold, and it slid across the ground towards him.

He took a second to kick it further away from the man's reach before he gripped the guy's shirt. Pulling him up to his feet, he plowed his fist into the man's face, knocking him to the ground again. Calvin rushed to him again and picked him up a second time.

Eddie fought to get free of Calvin's hold as a string of

curse words echoed in the now almost empty airport lobby. Calvin was working on pure adrenaline as they fell to the ground. His fists continued to plow into the man's face until he felt a hand on his shoulder.

"I think you've got him, son," an older black cop said as he stood over him. "Let us deal with him now."

Calvin glanced around and realized that Bella was sitting on the floor where she'd knocked Eddie to the ground. She was holding her left wrist and watching him with concern.

"He's a murderer," he told the cop. "He's wanted by the police for five murders. His name is Eddie Simons." He moved over to Bella. "Are you okay?" he asked, feeling his voice pitch.

"I think my arm is broken." She touched his face with her right hand. "You've got blood." She touched his lip and he felt the sting of where Eddie had gotten in a lucky punch to his lip.

"I'm okay," he assured her, then he ran his eyes over her. "The gun went off." He touched her face.

She glanced around and then motioned to one of the kiosks and laughed almost hysterically. "I think he only killed a machine this time."

"My god." He pulled her into his arms and kissed her.

He vaguely registered the claps and cheers of the bystanders as he held onto Bella. They sat on the airport floor and watched as the police handcuffed the unconscious Eddie. They had to wait for the ambulance to arrive, but he knew automatically that Bella's arm was indeed broken.

Eddie was hauled away shortly after he gained consciousness and instantly began to spew curse words and lies to the police. Shortly after Eddie was hauled away, Captain Elizabeth Feller arrived, just as they loaded Bella into the back of the ambulance.

Bella wanted to go to the hospital in a taxi, but the

captain convinced her to take the ride in the back of the ambulance instead.

"If you show up in a taxi, by the time you get there, every reporter will be waiting for you. The ambulance, with a police escort, will be there before the reporters get wind of what happened."

The captain even convinced them to allow him to ride along and assured them that their luggage would be delivered back to her apartment before the end of the day. He'd handed her over the baggage claims and somehow knew that he would never see his underwear again.

Hell, as long as Bella was safe, he didn't care.

The captain was wrong, though. When they rolled Bella out of the back of the ambulance, a string of paparazzi was already waiting for them.

"Damn," he growled as he tried to shield Bella.

"It's okay." She rested her head back and smiled up at him. "It's not me their taking pictures of. It's you. You're the hero that saved me."

He glanced over and sure enough, the cameras were pointed in his direction as questions were shouted at him.

There were questions directed at Bella too, but most of them were about how he'd singlehandedly taken down a killer with a gun at the airport.

He wanted to laugh at the vague description, but then realized that's exactly what had happened.

Bella was instantly moved into a private room. He was thankful for it, since he didn't want to deal with the group of people trying to get a picture of them.

They waited in the room until she could be rolled in for an X-ray.

He called Ben and filled him in as she rested back, holding her arm close to her chest.

"Hey," he said when Ben answered the phone.

"Hey, did you get on the plane yet?" Ben asked.

"No." He sighed. "Something came up. You might want to turn on the TV."

"Shit, what happened now?" Ben asked. Instantly, he heard Sarah in the background berate him about the language. "Sorry," Ben said to his wife, and Calvin heard his friend turn on the television in the background. Then Ben was silent as he watched the news report of what had happened at the airport. "Shit, man, are you and Bella okay?"

"Yes, your sister is alive and well."

"Hi, Ben," Bella called out with a smile. "I'm fine."

"We think she has a broken wrist. We're waiting in line for an X-ray. Other than that,"

"Calvin has a fat lip," Bella broke in.

"It's nothing." He frowned down at her.

"He took out a killer." She smiled up at him and reached with her good hand for his. "And I love him." She laughed.

"Okay, so they don't have her on drugs yet, but I think it's shock." He frowned down at her as he joked.

"My god. Do you know how many gray hairs you two have given me in the past few weeks?" Ben said. "Wow, there's footage of my sister tackling the ass—" Ben cleared his throat as Calvin heard Sarah complain again. "Sorry, the bastard down," Ben said with a chuckle.

"There is?" Calvin flipped on the television set and changed it to a news station and hit the mute button.

Sure enough, they watched as Bella tackled Eddie.

"What were you thinking?" Calvin asked Bella with a frown.

"I was thinking… he had a gun and could have just shot me." Her frown grew. "Or you."

He took a deep breath as the scene changed and suddenly, he saw himself rush over and pull the man up to his feet and then plow his fist into the guy's face.

"Okay," Ben said into his ear. "You win. You punch way better than I do."

Calvin couldn't help it, he laughed as he watched Eddie fold under his fists.

"Shit," he sighed as he watched himself lose control and continue to plow his fist into the unconscious man's face.

"Yeah, intense," Ben said in his ear. Then after a moment of silence Ben said, "Calvin?"

"Yeah?" He turned off the set and closed his eyes.

"Thanks for saving my sister."

"Any time." His eyes opened and landed on Bella, who was looking up at him like he was a superhero.

He waited almost an hour while her arm was x-rayed. A doctor confirmed it was broken at the wrist, and another nurse came in to put it in a cast.

He laughed at her when she picked pink as her cast color and watched the woman wrap the material around her entire arm to secure it.

Once it was done, he asked the nurse to borrow her pen. Leaning over Bella, he blocked her view as he worked on writing out his message to her.

"Marry me?" was spelled out in large letters so she could read it clearly.

When he finally let her see what he'd written, she laughed and nodded her head as she cried out, "Yes!" over and over again.

The nurse laughed and then relayed what had happened to several of her collogues.

Bella asked for the pen and wrote a large "YES" under his question.

Of course, at that point, word had gotten out that they had Bella Rothschild in the emergency room and requests for pictures ensued until they got her release papers.

He was slightly shocked that the nurses wanted his picture as well.

"You're as famous as she is," the older nurse had said. "After all, you're the one who took out the madman and saved the woman you love." She smiled up at him.

He felt a little foolish, but then he turned and saw the love in Bella's eyes and any strange feelings disappeared. He had the most important thing, the thing that mattered most to him, and she'd promised to be his forever.

EPILOGUE

*S*tanding on the pebble-ridden beach, she held the pink cast close to her body and took in the fresh air. She was finally home.

It seemed like it had taken years to get back here instead of two weeks.

When strong arms wrapped around her, she sighed and relaxed into a warm chest.

The weather was already turning and the leaves on all the trees were growing brighter. She'd missed the fall season so much. Now, it felt as if every feeling, every sense, she had was heightened.

She'd heard that near-death experiences could have that effect. But she knew it had nothing to do with what she'd gone through, but what she'd almost lost.

Watching Calvin rush towards Eddie that day, she'd had several moments of panic at the thought of the madman turning the gun on the man she loved.

She'd tackled Eddie not for herself, but for her future. The one she was going to build with Calvin, here, on this very spot.

She turned easily into his arms and wrapped her good arm around him as she looked up at the house, she now called home.

The home she planned on raising their kids in. The one she never wanted to leave for very long again.

She'd always wanted to sing, and she planned on continuing that dream, just as long as it didn't interfere with her new dream. Of being Mrs. Bella Winters.

"Happy?" he asked as he held her.

"Very," she answered with a sigh.

"Welcome home," he said just before he kissed her.

Breaking Travis

Roping Ryan

Wild Bride

Corey's Catch

Tessa's Turn

Saving Trace

The Grayton Series

Last Resort

Someday Beach

Rip Current

In Too Deep

Swept Away

High Tide

Lucky Series

Unlucky In Love

Sweet Resolve

Best of Luck

A Little Luck

Christmas Wish

Silver Cove Series

Silver Lining

French Kiss

Happy Accident

Hidden Charm

A Silver Cove Christmas

Sweet Surrender

Second Chances

Entangled Series – Paranormal Romance

The Awakening

The Beckoning

The Ascension

The Presence

The Calling

The Chosen

Haven, Montana Series

Closer to You

Never Let Go

Holding On

Coming Home

The Hard Way

Pride Oregon Series

A Dash of Love

My Kind of Love

Season of Love

Tis the Season

Dare to Love

Where I Belong

Because of Love

A Thing Called Love

First Comes Love

Someone to Love

Wildflowers Series

Summer Nights

Summer Heat

Summer Secrets

Summer Fling

Summer's End

Summer's Wish

Distracted Series

Wake Me

Tame Me

Stand Alone Books

Twisted Rock

Hope Harbor

Raven Falls

For a complete list of books:

http://JillSanders.com

Jill Sanders is a New York Times, USA Today, and international best-selling author of Sweet Contemporary Romance, Romantic Suspense, Western Romance, and Paranormal Romance novels. With over 70 books in eleven series, translations into several different languages, and audiobooks there's plenty to choose from. Look for Jill's bestselling stories wherever romance books are sold or visit her at jillsanders.com

Jill comes from a large family with six siblings, including an identical twin. She was raised in the Pacific Northwest and later relocated to Colorado for college and a successful IT career before discovering her talent for writing sweet and sexy page-turners. After Colorado, she decided to move south, living in Texas and now making her home along the Emerald Coast of Florida. You will find that the settings of several of her series are inspired by her time spent living in these areas. She has two sons and off-set the testosterone in her house by adopting three furry little ladies that provide her company while she's locked in her writing cave. She enjoys heading to the beach, hiking, swimming, wine-tasting, and pickle-ball with her husband, and of course writing. If you have read any of her books, you may also notice that there is a love of food, espe-

cially sweets! She has been blamed for a few added pounds by her assistant, editor, and fans... donuts or pie anyone?

Join Jill's Newsletter and get book and sales updates monthly. https://jillsanders.com/newsletter.html

Remember, if you've enjoyed this book, please leave a review where you downloaded it. Thanks

facebook.com/JillSandersBooks

twitter.com/JillMSanders

amazon.com/Jill-Sanders/e/B009M2NFD6?tag=jillmcom-20

bookbub.com/authors/jill-sanders

instagram.com/jillsandersauthor

www.ingramcontent.com/pod-product-compliance
Lightning Source LLC
Chambersburg PA
CBHW050833190726
48286CB00007B/2069